THREE TRUTHS
AND OTHER UNSETTLING TALES

Thomas O.

VELOX BOOKS
Published by arrangement with the author.

CONTENTS

THREE TRUTHS

The two men, perched on a steep hillside, watched from a safe distance as the invading army destroyed the city below them. The towering stone wall that protected the city, once strong and unbreakable, couldn't hold back the onslaught. Even over the sounds of war, the watchers could hear the yells of the invading commanders directing their soldiers. No man, woman, child, or beast was to be left alive. The instructions were carried out with swords and spears, and the slaughter was completed in the space of a day.

The two watchers, Danel and Keret, understood the implications of what they'd witnessed. The destroyed city was not the one from which they hailed. No, their city was the next closest, about a two day march away. Nearly a year earlier, along with several other soldiers, the two men had left their city on a mission to escort an ambassador to a faraway land. The mission had soured, and the ambassador was dead. On the return journey, the other soldiers had become victims of either the desert heat or nomadic attackers. Danel and Keret, the last survivors of the mission, were on their way home to report the failure of the undertaking. The two men had nearly stumbled, unexpectedly and accidentally, into the army of the invaders. It was an army from a land they weren't familiar with. Luckily for them, they remained undiscovered, but a return to their own city was beginning to look impossible. Half of the invading army had already marched off, even while the other half continued with the slaughter. Danel and Keret watched as the foreign soldiers headed toward their city, and they could hear the commanders talking their men up for yet another siege. They considered trying to get out ahead of the traveling invaders, so that maybe, just maybe, they could reach their city first to give warning. But the quickest route was through a small canyon, which was the same route the invaders were taking. They knew it would be impossible to follow that course and not be spotted. They chose a longer route, and hoped that the extra distance would be negated by the fact that two lonely men could travel faster than an invading army.

Upon their arrival, they found that they were too late—their city was already surrounded by the first half of the invasion force. Soon, the rest of them would arrive, and the attack would begin. Danel and Keret didn't have to discuss it, they both knew their city's fate would be the same as its neighbor. The invaders wanted this land for themselves, and their army was mightier than any they'd seen before. It seemed as if it was guided by an unstoppable force. The walls of their city would fall even faster than those of the city that came before.

They found a well-hidden position on a hillside, grimly observing the preparations unfolding down below them. "It's hopeless, we can do nothing for them," Keret lamented.

Danel rubbed a stone amulet that hung around his neck—a subconscious movement he made whenever he was deep in thought. Finally, he responded, "I won't leave her there. I can't just let her die with the rest of them." He looked down upon the doomed city he'd served faithfully. At a young age, he'd been ripped from his mother and given to the army. Trained to be a soldier, he was the property of the city itself. All of his life, he had followed pointless orders, fought in battles, and then followed even more pointless orders, never questioning his superiors or their motives.

As he surveyed the scene, he wasn't surprised that, save for one, he felt no concern or pity for the inhabitants he served. He had done all he could for them. Now, at the start of their inevitable demise, there was no sadness for the city itself, just a stoic acceptance.

Donatiya, his wife, was the only person for whom Danel spared concern. His battlefield heroics had allowed him the privilege of marrying her. Most of the soldiers weren't given that luxury. She was the only woman he had ever loved, and she was the only person who had ever loved him. His marriage, and his friendship with Keret, were the only two important relationships he'd ever formed.

Keret spoke, breaking Danel's concentration. "There's a way in, you know."

Danel averted his gaze from the city and looked at Keret. He was listening.

Keret continued, "The tunnel. I told you about it before, remember?"

Danel remembered. The ancient and forgotten tunnel ran from a hidden room underneath one of the city's temples and exited outside the walls at the base of a hill. Keret and his long-ago friends had explored the narrow space in their youth. Of that group, Keret was the only one still living. As for the tunnel, its outside entrance was hidden by a boulder, but two strong men could budge it just enough to crawl inside. Keret was unsure if anyone else even knew of its existence.

Keret's voice intensified. "We'll sneak in tonight. The entire army isn't here yet, so we should be able to make it past their lines." He pointed to a spot towards the southern end of the city, outside its wall, "Look there, what luck for us! They don't have many soldiers in that area. That's where the tunnel's entrance is, a small group could easily sneak in and out."

Both men studied the area, and Keret gave a wide smile and put his hand reassuringly on Danel's shoulder, "My friend, tonight we shall save your wife together."

Danel rubbed his amulet and responded, "Let's get some rest, we have much to accomplish." He was grateful that he had Keret with him, but he wondered how workable the plan really was.

At dusk, the two men laid themselves in the dirt, trying to get their first sleep in three days. Their plan was straightforward. They would wake up after the half-moon slipped below the horizon and sneak their way to the mouth of the entrance. They would quietly move the boulder aside and slip into the city. Once they were inside, nobody would bother them. They would retrieve Donatiya and slip back out.

Danel's sleep was fitful, and he dreamed of both Donatiya and a strange figure who stood behind her while she danced. The figure, a silhouette of a large man, had no distinguishable facial features. Donatiya danced around the figure, and Danel could tell the figure was watching her, even though he couldn't see its eyes.

Finally, the dark figure spoke to him. "I can help you save her." His voice made a hissing sound. Donatiya continued to dance seductively, and the figure repeated itself, "I can help you save her, but you must wake up now."

Danel opened his eyes. It was night—the starry sky and half-moon provided the only light. As he sat up, he saw the outline of the being he had just dreamt of standing right next to him. He made a grab for his sword.

"No!" the creature hissed. Danel felt an unseen force push his arm back down, away from his sword. "You will listen."

"Who are you?"

"I'm the one that you called upon." The entity remained featureless, even under the moonlight. A black arm extended from the darkness that enveloped the being, brushing a finger against the amulet hanging from Danel's neck.

Danel looked down at his amulet. "You are Baal?"

"Yessss," came the hissing response.

"I didn't call you here. I have no need of you." Danel was more nervous than his bold statement made him appear.

"Oh, but you did call me here. Every time you rub that object around your neck, you call out my name."

Danel glanced down at the amulet. He'd found the simple stone carving in the dirt several years earlier. At the time, he'd recognized that it was a depiction of Baal, one of the deities worshipped by his people. He began wearing it, not out of reverence, and not out of fear, but simply because it was something to wear, something that would distinguish him from the nameless soldiers with whom he shared ranks. The truth was, he'd always had very little use for the deities of his people. He didn't find it necessary to pray to them, and didn't feel the need to honor them. Before that night, he wasn't even sure they were real. Yet there he found himself, standing next to a creature that could only be a deity.

The visitor continued, "This plan of yours, to sneak into the city through a tunnel—this plan is foolish." The scorn in his voice was evident. "It will not succeed, and you will die. Keret will die. Donatiya will die."

Danel started to feel real fear for the first time in years. The legends involving Baal weren't pleasant. He didn't rule with benevolence, but used intimidation and fear to force people towards his will. He reveled in trickery and deceit. He bathed in blood and fed on sadness.

Baal's voice took a friendlier turn. "But you don't all have to die. I can get you into the city and out again. However, it will require a sacrifice on your part." With that last statement, he turned and looked at Keret, who was in a deep sleep.

A look of understanding slowly formed on Danel's face. "You want me to kill my friend?"

"I want his heart!" Baal said, as the hostility returned to his voice. "You'll look him in the eye, then you will cut into him and rip it out of his chest. Then you'll give it to me. In return, I will grant you the power to go into the city and safely retrieve one person of your choosing."

Slowly, Danel shook his head back and forth. "I won't do it. He's my only friend."

"Do you really think that you'll be able to sneak past that army? You will all die, but if you walk the path I set out for you, then only he dies."

Danel agonized over the choice. The more he considered Keret's plan, the more he came to believe that it was a fool's errand that could only end in tragedy. The dark figure stood patiently while Danel debated himself in torment. Finally, his pragmatic nature, and his training as a soldier, led him to make the difficult decision.

"I'll sacrifice my friend to you, and I'll give you his heart, but first, you must grant me three truths before I commit." Danel couldn't bring himself to look at the entity as he spoke.

"Three truths. Of course. You would be a fool not to ask that of me." It seemed as if the figure might've smiled as he said those words.

Danel had been well versed in the legends and superstitions of his people, even though he never had too much faith in them. The tradition of the three truths specified that a person, before making a pact with a deity, could ask three questions. If the deity agreed to answer, it would be unable to lie. The one limitation of the questions was that they had to be asked in a manner that could be answered with a simple yes or no, though the legend held that the deity could provide additional information if it chose to. The priests of Danel's city swore this to be true, and the man, formerly of little faith, was about to put their teachings to the test.

Danel took a moment to compose his thoughts. He knew there was a good chance Baal was involved in some sort of trickery, and it was possible that nothing he'd said up to that point was true. He had to ask smart questions. A sudden, sinking feeling fell upon him as he thought to himself that Donatiya might have already passed away in his absence.

"My first question, is Donatiya still alive?"

Baal nodded his head. "Yes. She is alive. She is healthy. She's in your home, yearning for you."

Danel was relieved at the answer, and pleasantly surprised at the extra information Baal had provided. "My second question, were you honest when you said that you'll provide me with the ability to enter the city and safely leave with Donatiya?

Again, Baal nodded. "Yes, so long as you give me your friend's heart. You can leave with Donatiya, or perhaps your father, or maybe your brother. You can pick anyone in the city."

Danel wanted to smile but held back. Now I understand his trickery, he thought. He thinks I care for my father and brother. He thinks I'm going to have a difficult time choosing who to take.

Baal didn't appear to know that Danel hated both his father and his brother. His father was the one who'd ripped him away from his mother and sold him to the army. He barely knew his brother, but he did know that he was an awful man who wasn't worthy of saving. The choice would be easy, very easy, but he didn't want an emotional expression to betray him to Baal. He forced a look of turmoil upon his face.

Feeling more confident in the path Baal had laid out for him, his concern turned back to Keret. He knew that people sacrificed to Baal were often killed in the most excruciating ways possible. "My third question, you told me that you wanted Keret's heart cut out. That could be long and painful for him. Will you allow him a quick death?"

"Yes, I will allow you to give him a quick death. You may choose any means of execution, so long as you don't damage the heart."

Danel hung his head in relief.

Baal hissed again, "You have your three truths. Now go get me his heart!"

Danel turned and faced the spot where Keret had been sleeping, only to find him sitting up awake.

"How long have you been awake?" he demanded.

Keret didn't answer the question, but instead made his own inquiry. "What was that thing you were talking to?"

Danel looked to where Baal had been only a moment earlier, but the deity was gone. He turned back and tried to look at Keret, but ended up averting his eyes. "I… I made a deal with him."

"I've seen that thing before. That was Baal, wasn't it? This is serious my friend, you shouldn't make deals with him."

"Yes Keret. It was Baal. He granted me three truths. I can save Donatiya. I know that for sure."

"But we can do that together! We don't need him."

"No, he told me our plan would fail. He told me we would all die."

Keret shook his head, "That's wrong. It's a good plan. I must ask, when he told you it wouldn't work, was that one of the three truths?"

Danel felt as if he'd been punched in the gut. He didn't answer.

"Danel, listen to me. I've lived longer than you, and I've traveled farther. I've learned much, and I know that Baal is no deity, he's one of the fallen. The pathway of Baal is the pathway to sorrow. He has no loyalty, not even to those who serve him."

Danel didn't want to argue with Keret anymore. He saw no point. He knew the truth. He could save Donatiya, and that was all that mattered anymore.

"He wants your heart. I'm sorry."

A look of rage filled Keret's face. "He wants my heart? Here, take it if you think that's what you really need!"

He stood up, pulled his sword out, then threw it to the ground. "Go ahead now, do what you need to!"

Danel drew his sword and shut down his emotions, as he'd been trained to do.

Keret continued with his rage, hitting his fist against his chest. "Take it! I won't stop you! Just rip it out!"

Danel's sword lashed out right as Keret finished his final sentence. The very last expression on his face was a look of surprise, as if he hadn't really expected Danel to strike him. Keret's head flew off his body and landed in a ditch several feet away.

For a moment, Danel fell to his knees in sorrow. The pain of his actions nearly overwhelmed him, but he thought back to the lessons of his youth. For one last time, he pushed his personal feelings aside so that he could complete his mission. The emotions weren't suppressed easily, but none-the-less, Danel regained his focus. Drawing his knife, he sliced into Keret's belly and up into his rib cage. After several minutes of cutting and tugging, he retrieved the heart of his friend.

The hissing voice sounded out behind him, "Make a fire and blacken the heart. I will tell you when it's done."

"I'll give my location away if I make a fire," Danel protested.

"Do not worry about that, I will make sure they don't see you."

Danel made a fire, as instructed, and placed the heart upon it. Behind him, Baal chanted in an unknown language. The heart burned on the fire until well after the moon went down. The night became even darker.

"You may take the heart off the fire now," Baal instructed.

Danel used some sticks and placed the heart upon a large rock.

Baal nodded his approval. "Use your knife, and make a slit in the heart."

Once the slit was made, bright red blood gushed from within and dripped down onto the rock.

"Now, smear some of the blood onto your forehead. You'll be able to walk into the city undetected. The blood will remain wet. When you select the person you want to bring back, smear some of the blood onto their forehead. You will both be able to leave safely. Remember, you can choose only one, otherwise a punishment worse than death will befall anyone who has been touched by the blood. The invaders will attack at midday, you must leave the city before then. Now go, and leave the heart here for me."

After smearing a generous amount of blood on his forehead, Danel walked from the hill toward the city. To take his mind off of the death of Keret, he imagined what his future life would be like with Donatiya. He knew of several cities that would take them in, it was one of the advantages of being well traveled. He imagined them both living in a small house far from the invaders. She would give him a son, and his son would grow up with the love and privilege that he himself had never received. They would have many children, and he would no longer be pressed into the service of the army.

As he approached the first set of night watch soldiers, he paused and took a deep breath. Their torches burned brightly in the darkness, but they didn't seem to notice him. As he closed in, they stopped moving entirely, as if they were frozen in place. Walking past them, he turned around and continued to eye them. As the distance between Danel and the soldiers increased, the soldiers slowly started moving again, oblivious to the fact that an enemy had just walked by them.

Relieved, his mind began to wander again. He hadn't seen his wife in ages, it seemed. He wondered if she would look different. He thought about how happy she would be to see him, and he smiled at the thought.

He finally reached the main gate of the city. The guards on duty looked down on him from high on the wall with vacant stares on their faces. They opened the gate for him without saying a word. Even though the gate was completely open, none of the invaders seemed to notice. Danel walked into the city, and the gate closed behind him.

His heart beat faster. He broke into a run, trying to get to his small wooden hovel as fast as possible. The people of the city looked worried. They were crying and arguing. Soldiers were busy fortifying their positions along the wall. Nobody gave any attention to Danel as he ran through the alleys. Out of breath, he burst through the door of his home.

Donatiya was awake in bed when he entered. A single lantern illuminated the room. "Danel!" She screamed out his name in joy as he ran toward her. She looked exactly as he remembered her.

They embraced and kissed. He held her close for several moments. He couldn't begin to explain to her how he managed to get there, and she didn't ask, she just accepted his presence happily.

Danel looked into her eyes. "I came back here to save you. We must leave now."

"That makes me so happy," she said, "But wait, there's something wonderful I must show you!" She moved over to the bed and picked up a small bundle of blankets that he hadn't noticed earlier. She approached him with a smile as he heard a small cry emanate from within the bundle.

Inside, he saw a baby, perhaps three months old.

"Meet your son," Donatiya beamed.

Danel looked at the baby, and his heart filled with love and pride. The small child, conceived in the days before he left, and birthed in his absence, had the same color eyes as him. Donatiya handed the bundle to him, and he held his first and only son closely. However, his smile faded, and his pride quickly turned into horror as he realized the true extent of Baal's evilness. Looking at Donatiya and the baby, he remembered what Baal had told him, "Remember, you can choose only one!"

He knew the choice would be impossible.

He knew the choice would be impossible.

BZZZ

Calvin felt something vibrate deep within his skull. It was the most unnatural feeling he could imagine, almost like he had some sort of buzzer buried between the lobes of his brain. He shot up in bed, and after a moment of confusion, he decided he'd dreamed it, as it was nearly two in the morning. He rolled up next to Tabitha and allowed himself to relax.

They were two-hundred miles beyond nowhere. Tabitha had dragged Calvin far into the wilderness to meet her father, a recluse who spent his summers in a remote Alaskan cabin. Their trek in had been long, flying over the trees in what was probably the world's oldest bushmaster. Hooper Jacobs, a man whose proudest achievements were being both a former minor league ballplayer and Tabitha's father, had wanted to meet Calvin. More importantly, he wanted to see just how far Calvin would be willing to go to please his daughter. Would he really travel all the way to the wild outreaches of Alaska? He had. Calvin passed the test, at least the first part of it.

Exhausted from their long journey, the two travelers had eaten a quick meal and then went right to bed, hoping to take advantage of the three hours of darkness they could expect. Calvin slept well, right up to the point when the buzzing in his head woke him up.

Back in the confines of Tabitha's embrace, sleep found him once more. An hour later, as the morning sun rose, the two woke up still tired from their journey. They managed to get dressed and exit the cabin's sole bedroom, which had kindly been loaned to them by Hooper.

Over breakfast, Hooper started in with the inevitable get-to-know-you banter. "So, Tabitha tells me you're an engineer," the older man said.

"Yes," Calvin replied. He tried to elaborate further, wanting to describe the latest ten-lane overpass he'd worked on, yet he suddenly realized that he couldn't remember any specifics. It was as if they'd been wiped from his brain. He trailed off as he mentally grasped for a fact, any fact, that might make his job seem interesting.

"How long have you been doing that?" Hooper asked, without seeming to notice the fact that Calvin was still trying to add to his previous answer.

"Uh," Calvin's brow furrowed as he went into deep thought, "I don't really know." He gave a nervous laugh at his sudden inability to come up with an answer to such a simple question.

Tabitha butted in. "Stop being silly!" She playfully hit Calvin's arm, then looked at her father. "He's been working there for five years. They hired him right out of college," she said proudly.

Calvin chuckled along with Tabitha as he scratched an itchy spot on the back of his neck. "Yep," he agreed, "five years." Calvin relaxed, and there were no other memory hiccups for him that morning. Soon, Hooper began warming to Calvin.

It wasn't until that evening that Calvin felt the buzzing again, this time while the three sat on the outdoor deck eating dinner. Lasting for several seconds, the violent vibration emanated deep from within his skull and tickled the back of his eyeballs. This came just as Hooper was telling him about the homerun he once hit over the wall in Skeldon Stadium. "The furthest ball ever hit there," he bragged.

Calvin jerked up. "What was that?" he exclaimed.

Tabitha and Hooper both gave him an odd look.

"The buzzing," he clarified. "Did anyone else feel that?"

"You must be hearing things," Tabitha said with a laugh. "Probably just a fly."

Calvin swatted the empty space in front of him, attempting to ward off a pest he wasn't so sure existed.

"Yeah, the flies up here are monsters," Hooper stated with authority.

Calvin tuned the others out, waiting for the buzzing again, but after a few moments it seemed that the affliction had passed. A general feeling of unease settled over him. That was two times now that he felt the mysterious vibration. It was distracting to say the least, but becoming worrisome the more he thought about it. He put it out of his mind and carried on for the rest of the night, convincing himself that everything was okay.

The next day Hooper took them fishing, which proved to be fruitful. The sun was still bright in the sky as they ate their catch outside the cabin. Tabitha was explaining how, when she was young, Hooper had always tried to teach her about baseball. "And I swear to God that I had no interest in learning any of that…"

Calvin's ears vibrated. "Damn it!" he interrupted as he jumped up from the table. "I think I have a bug in my ear!" He felt around the outside of his ear, then jammed his pinky inside, hoping that he'd find the culprit.

Tabitha had a piece of fish sticking out of her mouth. "Do you feel anything?" she asked.

"No. I don't think so." He wiggled his finger back and forth in his ear, still agitated.

Tabitha laughed at the absurdity of Calvin trying to fish a bug out of his ear, while Hooper resumed the conversation they'd been having. "Calvin, you were telling me about California," he said in his booming voice.

Calvin pulled his finger from his ear and looked at him, puzzled. "California?"

"Yeah, you were telling me you grew up there."

"Grew up…" Calvin faded off.

Tabitha's smile lowered. "Calvin, you look like you're lost at sea."

Calvin scratched the back of his neck in a daze. "What's this?" he asked as his finger passed over a bump that his longish brown hair just barely covered. His fugue seemed to clear.

Hooper put his fork down as he leaned in closer to look at the spot where Calvin was lifting up his hair. "Looks infected maybe."

Tabitha also leaned in closer. "Oh gross, Calvin! It looks like some sort of bug bite, but it's huge. Look, Dad, it's got some pus coming out of it." She reached her hand over to the back of Calvin's neck and pushed the bump with her pinky. "Gross," she said again as she wiped her finger on a napkin.

"Maybe we should have someone look at that," Hooper said as he shot a concerned look at his daughter. "There's a retired doctor who lives about five miles from here. Name's Hecht. He might have something to say about it."

Calvin protested. "No, I think it's fine. It's probably just a mosquito bite."

"Calvin," Hooper stated, "up around here people call mosquitoes the Alaskan state bird. I've seen a million mosquito bites, and that wasn't done by a mosquito."

Calvin reached around for a second time and poked the bump on his neck. Tabitha grimaced as more pus oozed from the reddened area. "You should really go, babe," she said.

"I'll radio him," Hooper said, "let him know we're coming." Hooper glanced at the sky. "We're not going to get too much in the way of darkness tonight. We shouldn't waste it. Get some sleep and we'll head over there in the morning."

That night, Tabitha was woken by the sound of Calvin's palm slapping against the back of his own head. "Something's in there!" he screamed.

"What? What is it?" Tabitha shot up.

"It's inside my head." Calvin said, "Whatever's doing that buzzing, it's inside of me."

Tabitha sat up and comforted Calvin, slowly massaging his shoulders. "Maybe we should just get you to a hospital as soon as possible."

"I think I'll be okay."

"No, we need to get you some help."

"I'll see Dr. Hecht later today. He'll help me."

Tabitha continued with her argument. "I don't think that'll be good enough."

"If Dr. Hecht tells me I need to go to a hospital, then I'll go."

"Maybe we shouldn't have even come up here. What was I thinking? Dragging you away from civilization like this. Next time my dad wants to see me, he needs to come visit us, just like your mom did."

Calvin paused for a moment, as if he was deep in thought. "My mom?" he asked. "Who is my mom?"

"Are you serious?" She sat stone-faced as she waited for his response.

"I can't remember."

Tabitha smiled in desperation, waiting for it to all be a joke, but the furrow on Calvin's brow didn't waver. She got out of bed and retrieved her bra from the floor. "Okay, that's it. We're getting you to a hospital, now. I'll have Dad drive us back to the airstrip." She maneuvered her arms and shoulders through the bra-straps, then found her shorts on the floor and put them on. She grabbed her crumpled t-shirt off the nightstand as she left the bedroom to wake her father.

Hooper listened as Tabitha asked him to return them to the airstrip. "He's got to go, Dad. It's an emergency. First it was the buzzing, and now he's having trouble remembering things," she said.

"It'll take a while to get a pilot out here. Let's see Hecht first and see what he says." Hooper looked out the dark window. "We'll leave at first light. Start getting ready."

The ride over the bumpy dirt road jolted the three occupants of the four-seat ATV, and even though they only traveled five miles, the journey seemed to take far too long. As they arrived, Tabitha saw a man who appeared to be in his mid-sixties step out of the cabin. He ushered them right in, not being one for pleasantries.

Dr. Hecht directed Calvin to sit down on a chair and then asked him to describe the buzzing that he was feeling. With gloved hands, he examined the bump on the back of Calvin's neck. It was Tabitha who told him about the memory lapses Calvin had been suffering.

Dr. Hecht questioned him. "What's your full name?"

"Calvin Evan Roberts."

"What's the date today?"

Calvin answered quickly and correctly.

"Where are you at?"

"Alaska."

"Where did you meet Tabitha?"

Calvin remained silent as his eyes shifted upward in an attempt to recall the information.

"Calvin?" Tabitha's sweet voice cooed. "Don't you remember?" It was an excruciating half minute for Tabitha as she watched the man she loved struggle to recall how they met.

"Economics class," he finally said. "I think."

"Tell me about your family," Dr. Hecht said. "What are their names?"

Calvin looked downward. "I know my mother loves me. I remember being happy."

"But do you remember her name?" the doctor asked as he looked into Calvin's eyes.

Calvin shook his head. "I can't even remember what she looks like."

The same held true for the rest of Calvin's family. Tabitha's stomach dropped every time Calvin failed to recall what should've come easily to him.

Dr. Hecht ended his line of questioning with a shake of his head. "I don't know what I can do for you out here, Calvin."

"What do you think is wrong with him?" Tabitha asked.

"Well, his short-term memory is fine. It's his long-term memories that seem to be missing. Then there's that wound on his neck, and the buzzing that he's feeling. I'm at a loss. There's really nothing I know of that would cause all of these symptoms…"

Tabitha noticed a hesitancy in the doctor's voice, and guessed that he was withholding something. "Except for…" she led.

Dr. Hecht gave a smirk of acknowledgement. "This daughter of yours is quick on the uptake, Hooper." He looked back at Tabitha. "Except for an insane hypothesis that probably isn't true."

"Tell us, Hecht," Hooper insisted.

"Just keep in mind that what I'm about to tell you is probably batshit crazy. It's just something that a couple of the old-timers told me when I first moved up here, and I didn't put too much stock into it until now."

Tabitha sat down.

"I don't even know where to start with this, but it's a bug, a particularly nasty one that nests in the human brain."

"You mean like a bacteria?" Calvin asked.

"No, I mean an insect. A big one, something like a hornet."

Tabitha shook her head. "There are no hornets that nest in the human brain."

"I didn't say it was a hornet. I said it was similar to one, or at least I've been told that's what it looks like. The adult plants an egg at the stem of the brain, then the larva works its way inside, where it grows." He looked directly at Calvin. "If this is what's afflicting you, you probably got bit right after your plane landed."

"How come I've never heard of anything like this before?" Tabitha demanded.

Dr. Hecht threw his hands up in resignation. "Like I said, I'm not even sure I believe it myself. The old guys, they say it's on a thirty-year cycle. These things show up maybe twice in a lifetime and stick around only for a few months. And even then, there's probably only a handful of them."

"So, these things, where do they go when they disappear?" Calvin asked as he rubbed the side of his head.

"I don't know, son." Dr. Hecht said. "Maybe they hibernate, or maybe they go underground like the cicadas do."

Calvin felt the bug buzz again, the strongest one yet. Tabitha, who was the closest to Calvin, yelled in surprise. "I heard it!" she shouted as she pointed at the side of Calvin's head.

Calvin hit the side of his head with his palm. "Get it out!" he screamed as he rocked back and forth.

Tabitha dropped her arm and embraced Calvin. "Oh God, babe. It's true." Tears welled up in her eyes. She held onto Calvin as Dr. Hecht ushered her father outside to speak privately.

Tabitha held him close until Dr. Hecht and her father finally returned. Hooper looked solemn. "There's a clinic over in Banshee that I've gone to before," he began. "It's the closest medical facility, but Dr. Hecht thinks you should go straight to Anchorage."

Dr. Hecht chimed in, "It's further, but you'll get far better care there." The doctor nodded toward his satellite phone. "I'll arrange for a pilot to pick you up at the airstrip."

Calvin nodded his agreement. Tabitha's stomach fell as she noticed the grimness with which he did so.

Leaving Dr. Hecht's place, the three climbed into Hooper's ATV and drove off. "Calvin," Hooper said, "I believe in telling the absolute truth, always. So I'm going to tell you what the doc told me about this bug that might be in your brain."

"Uh, dad. Don't scare us."

"No," said Calvin, "I want to know what I can expect."

"This thing is feeding on your brain," he said bluntly.

"Is that why he can't seem to remember anything?" Tabitha asked.

"Yeah, that's what the doc thinks. It seems like this thing is lodged in the area responsible for some of his long-term memories."

"It's eating my memories. My whole life." Calvin looked forlorn.

"Eventually," Hooper continued, "it will have to make its way out of your head."

Tabitha shuddered at the thought. She looked at Calvin, the man she loved, and gently caressed his cheek.

The ride over the unpaved road was difficult, but they arrived at the airstrip in two hours. They were the only ones there. "It might still be awhile, maybe even up to a day," Hooper said. He looked at Calvin, who was getting paler by the minute. "You know, there's a cabin about a mile further down. I know the guy who owns it. He's gone a lot, and he won't mind if you two wait there. You'll be far more comfortable than if you wait here." Hooper pulled his ATV back onto the dirt road. "I'll drop you off and then come back here to make sure we don't miss anything."

The three proceeded to the cabin. By the time they got there, Calvin had already grown noticeably weaker. Hooper helped him into the single room dwelling. He stumbled in and fell onto the bed, sweating and breathing heavily. Sitting on the bed next to him, Tabitha ran her fingers through his hair to comfort him.

"Look after him, I hope it won't be too long," came Hooper's voice as he exited and closed the door behind him. A few seconds later, the sound of his tires rolling over the rocks and gravel echoed through the cabin. The sound grew fainter, and they were alone.

Calvin writhed as he felt the bug move around his brain again. Tabitha reflexively covered her ears and cringed when she heard it. To her, it sounded like an angry bee stuck inside a plastic bag, only lower pitched. "Does it hurt?" she asked.

"Actually, no." Calvin pondered for a moment, then added, "It's a very uncomfortable feeling, but it doesn't really hurt."

Tabitha laid herself next to Calvin and placed her arm across his chest. She closed her eyes and rested.

Some time later, she awoke to hear Calvin whispering to himself. "My mother is Norma. She was kind to me when I was growing up. I have a brother named Tim. He used to pick on me when we were little, but I know he loved me."

He repeated the same phrase several times before Tabitha interrupted. "What are you saying, babe?" she said in a whisper.

Tabitha's words came as a surprise, and he stopped his spiel mid-sentence. "I was able to remember a few things after all. I don't want to lose them again. I can already feel them fading."

"It's like you're moving those things from your long-term memory to your short-term memory."

Calvin gave a genuine smile. "That's why I love you, Tab, because you get me."

He laid his head back down and closed his eyes, continuing his words. "My mother is Norma, she loved me. My brother is Tim. He used to pick on me when we were little, but I know he loved me. My father is…" There was a long pause. "My father is… God damn it!"

"Your father is Clyde. You two weren't really that close, but he was a good man. You told me that one of your best memories of him was the time he took you to the Dodgers game on opening day and you sat right behind third base."

"I don't remember that at all." Calvin covered his face with his hand.

"You caught a foul ball. You still have it on your dresser at home."

Calvin nodded and then resumed his whispering. "My mother is Norma. She was always good to me. My brother is Tim, he picked on me but loved me. My father is Clyde, he took me to a baseball game, and I caught a foul ball.

Tabitha held Calvin closer as he continued to repeat facts about his childhood. Her eyes watered as she said a little prayer that Calvin would never forget her, then she drifted off back to sleep.

BZZZZZ—The buzzing was loud enough to wake Tabitha, and she jerked up. Calvin was holding both hands to his head so hard that his fingers were white from the pressure. He sprang up from the bed and ran across the room. He pulled his head back and then slammed it against the wall. "Get out of my fucking head!" he screamed.

Tabitha jumped up after Calvin and grabbed him. "Calvin! Stop!" she said as she pushed herself between the man and the wall. "No more," she cried, "that won't do anything except hurt you."

Calvin held her close and cried on her shoulder. She supported his weight and helped him walk back to the bed where he collapsed. He caught his breath and spoke, "This thing, it's perfect."

"What do you mean?"

"I mean that if I designed evil bugs instead of bridges, this is exactly what I'd aspire to." His deep, rhythmic breathing continued. "Think about it. It can sting without its victim even feeling it. There's no way to remove the larvae without killing the host. It slowly incapacitates its victims so that when it's time for it to emerge, there won't be a fight. And wow, it must release some sort of endorphin or natural painkiller, because I feel fucking great right now." He gave a maniacal laugh, which made him sound like he was feeling anything but great.

"We're going to get this thing out of you, Calvin."

"I doubt that. Your dad hasn't checked back yet, and it's starting to get dark. I don't think a plane is going to land here after sunset."

"It won't be dark for long. I bet a plane will be here first thing in the morning," Tabitha said as she turned on a battery-powered lantern that was on the table.

"I think my brain will be mush before then. I can't fight it." He gave another high-pitched laugh. "Just let it happen."

"Let what happen? Let it erase who you are?"

"Yeah, that. And let it kill me."

She walked back to him and grabbed him by the shoulders. "Listen to me, this bug is not going to kill you!"

"Well, what do you think will happen when it emerges? Do you think that's something I can survive? I can feel it when it moves. It's heavy now, like an iron ball bouncing around my head. I don't know how it's going to come out, but I know it's not going to be pretty."

"Keep your spirits up, okay?

Calvin laid on his back, smiling. "It will probably take the path of least resistance. Maybe through my eye socket, or through my ear. Maybe through the sinuses and out my mouth." He stared at the ceiling. "My mother's name is… My mother's name is…"

"Norma."

"Yeah, Norma."

"Your father is Clyde and your brother is Tim."

"If you say so."

Tabitha sat up and faced him. "Don't give up! Your life is worth fighting for. I'll show you." She slowly moved her hand towards the fly of his pants, where she rubbed it against a slowly growing bulge.

Tabitha saw that his eyes showed a little sparkle. He grinned and spoke. "My girlfriend's name is Tabitha. I love her. She's worth fighting for."

"I love you too," she said as she lowered his zipper. Calvin closed his eyes and relaxed.

More time passed. Tabitha, snuggled up next to Calvin, felt him nudge her. She raised her head and looked at Calvin. "It's happening," he said.

She saw that Calvin's left eye was bulging outward. "Oh my God, Calvin!" she shrieked. "What should I do?"

"I don't know. I can't see," he said.

His eye bulged further outward as he let out a horrible scream. Suddenly, a volcano of blood and vitreous fluid splattered over Tabitha as the contents of Calvin's eye erupted from his head. In revulsion, she screamed and jumped away as a black and yellow bug unfurled itself from within the crater where Calvin's eye had been. The bug, which seemed almost too big to have emerged from an eye socket, shook fluid off of itself with a mighty vibration that sounded like a thousand angry bees. It spread out its legs and crawled across Calvin's face.

Tabitha looked around in desperation for an object she could use to smash the six-legged bastard. In the corner she spotted a fireplace poker. It was her best bet. She bounded across the room and retrieved the weapon, intent on using it to smash the newly spawned creature.

The bug perched itself over Calvin's mouth as Tabitha approached. She brought the poker up over her head, but knew she'd be unable to bring it down as long as that thing was on Calvin's face. She hesitated, unsure what to do, when the thing launched itself off of Calvin and flew toward her. She dodged the bug as it glanced off of her cheek, leaving a trail of Calvin's blood smeared over her face.

Off balance, she dropped the poker. The bug flew up to the rafters and buzzed its wings, while the sound reverberated off the walls and made it impossible to tell its exact location.

Tabitha glanced at Calvin, whose shallow breaths were coming at increasingly longer intervals. She turned her attention to the rafters. "Okay you son of a bitch." Reaching into her jeans pocket, she pulled out a hair-tie and used it to clear her hair from her face. She bent at the knees and retrieved the poker. "I'm down here."

From the corner of her eye, she saw a black and yellow blur as the bug zipped down from the rafters and closed in on her. She thought back to her youth, when her father taught her how to swing a baseball bat. She never really cared for the game, but the lesson stuck with her. She stepped into her swing and barely missed the bug as it angrily flew by. Her momentum threw her off balance, and she fell to her knee. The bug flew across the room and then zipped back around to make a second pass. She dove to the ground as it buzzed right over her head.

Grasping the poker tightly, she got back to her feet and readied herself for another pass, but the bug had disappeared somewhere in the cabin. She moved in a circle as she looked for the creature, but the dim light of the single lantern meant that the bug could be hidden almost anywhere. Her mind was racing. *Does this thing even need to find a mate before it plants an egg?* she wondered.

She paused to consider her options, and at that moment, she felt an almost imperceptible tickle on the back of her neck. Her free hand shot up and pushed the bug away. It flew back up to the rafters, buzzing angrily. Tabitha, in a panic, felt for an entry wound on the back of her neck, but breathed a quick sigh when she found that her skin was intact.

The bug had no intention of stopping, and again it flew down and headed directly at her. She had just enough time to step to the side and swing the poker. This time she connected, and with the most satisfying smash ever, the bug exploded into a mess of goo, wings, and legs. The insect's stinger shot out across the room and stuck into the wall with a dull thud.

Tabitha dropped the poker and ran over to Calvin, who was struggling to breathe. "We did it, babe! We got it!" She grabbed his hand. "Your name is Calvin Roberts. Your mother is Norma. You had a happy childhood and a good life," she said, wiping the tears from her face.

Calvin squeezed her hand in acknowledgment.

"And you have a girlfriend who loves you," she said.

He squeezed her hand for the last time, and then took his final breath.

MAGDA

As a child, I lived with my parents in Biltfort Manor, a home that dates back to 1897. It's probably the nicest house you'll ever see. I could go on and on about how beautiful it is, but the splendor of the home isn't important to this story. What you really need to know is that there's a feature on the grounds that, as far as I know, isn't replicated anywhere else. You see, a few years after the manor was built, the Biltfort family started a tradition that still carries on to this day—they planted their Christmas tree outside the manor house when Christmas was over. The trick to doing this successfully is that you have to get a tree with its root ball still intact. This first tree, the "1901" tree, is rooted right next to the house. About twenty feet away from that tree is—you guessed it— the "1902" tree. As the years went by, each new tree was planted a little bit further along. The effect is that as someone pulls off the main highway, they'll follow a line of evenly spaced pine trees that get older and grander as they get closer to the manor. Some of the trees are quite huge. The Biltforts owned the manor through two generations, finally selling it in 1952. The new owners fell in love with the Christmas tree tradition and continued on with it. My family bought the home in the late 70s, and we too kept up with the tradition.

I loved staring out the car window at the line of trees every time my parents and I drove up to the house. Each one had its own history and unique personality. When I was feeling bored, I'd go outside and run alongside them. Sometimes, I'd even use a stop-watch to see how long it took me to make it to the farthest tree and back (three and a half minutes, by the way). It was during one of those runs that I first noticed something was amiss—there was an extra-large gap between two of the trees. It was as if another tree should've been between them, but wasn't. Most people probably wouldn't have given a second thought to the apparently missing tree, but to me it was a mystery in my very own front yard, and I dwelled on it all day long, wondering what possibly could've happened to it.

Fueled by my curiosity, I counted the number of trees between the house and the missing pine—I got fifty-seven, which meant that "1958" was unaccounted for. I pointed it out to my father later that evening. He took a walk with me before sunset and confirmed that yes, a tree did, in fact, appear to be absent.

"I wonder what happened to it," I said as I stood in the exact spot where it should've been.

"I dunno, Champ. Maybe it got sick and died."

I laughed at that. "Trees don't get sick!"

"Sure they do. Lots of things can make a tree sick. Or maybe it even got hit by lightning."

"Well, I want to know for sure!" I demanded. At that same moment, I felt a sudden chill pass through my body. It started at my feet and worked its way up. I shuddered, not knowing why I was doing so.

My father didn't seem to notice. "I don't think we'll ever know for sure, Charlie. Sometimes that's just how it is." The sun was starting to set, so together we walked back to the manor house.

The mystery bothered me for months, right up until Christmas Eve, when *the dead man* came to visit me—and that's where this story really begins. It was late, several hours after my parents and I had enjoyed our Christmas Eve feast. I was trying to fall asleep when I noticed, by the pale green light of my digital clock, that someone was standing at the foot of my bed. I had no idea how he'd gotten inside.

My heart nearly tore out of my chest. I feigned sleep in hope that the man wouldn't hurt me, but he wasn't deceived. "You can get out of bed," he said with a drawl.

My eyes peeked open, but my body didn't move.

"Get up!" he insisted as he violently pulled my comforter from the bed with his dirty hands. I sat up shakily, all while planning to run off to my parents' bedroom once the opportunity presented itself.

"Don't think about goin' runnin' to your parents now," the man said. He wasn't very tall, but his dark, stabbing eyes peered past his greasy, long hair and made him more menacing than any giant could've been. "Yeah, that's right. I'm in your head. I know exactly what you're thinkin'." He grabbed my shirt and lifted me to my feet. "What do you want for Christmas?" he asked.

Fear drove away my ability to speak.

"Fine, don't tell me," the man said with a laugh. "I already know what you asked for."

I reflexively ran through my Christmas list in my mind… an Atari, a basketball, a racetrack…

"Boy, you ain't gettin' an Atari from me," he twanged. "But you want to know about that missing Christmas tree out front, don't you?"

Still holding onto my shirt, the man walked me out of the room. He didn't even flinch as I screamed out for my parents. They didn't respond, which didn't seem to surprise him at all. I later figured that he'd used some sort of charm that kept them asleep, though I know they would've fought tooth-and-nail to save me if they could've.

We made it outside to the front of the manor, where an unfamiliar car was parked. I can't tell you the make or model, but it was a shiny white muscle car straight from the 1970s. He left me standing there as he went around to the driver's side and stepped in.

He looked over at me through the side window. "Get in," he demanded. The passenger door opened on its own.

I shook my head slowly as I backed away. Only a minute earlier I'd been resting snug in my bed, yet there I stood in the cold outdoors being given directions by a psychopath. Everything was happening so fast.

"Boy," the man drawled, "if I have to get back out of this car to collect you, I'm going to cut your fuckin' tongue out."

I took another step backwards and slipped on slush and gravel, landing square on my ass. I heard his door open as I stood up and tried to run, but in only a few seconds he was upon me. He reached into his waistband and pulled out a switchblade that opened with a single fluid movement. "Now you've pissed me off, kid!" he said as he jammed his fingers into my mouth and pinched my tongue. I shook my head ferociously, trying to free myself. He made a fist with his other hand and punched the side of my head. "I'm just gonna keep clockin' you if you don't relax," he spat out.

I was stunned into obedience. The man pinched his fingers down hard and pulled my tongue out past my lips, further than I ever realized it could extend. The knife glinted in the moonlight as he raised it up and started slicing into the side of my exposed tongue like it was a piece of veal. If you've ever bitten your tongue before, multiply that pain by a thousand and you'll know how I felt in that moment. Just as I thought I was about to lose my tongue forever, the man stopped mid-slice and threw the knife to the ground in anger. It sizzled as it landed in the snow.

"God damn it!" he screamed. "Just look what you made me do." The blood ran freely from my mouth. The man reached into his back pocket and threw an oily rag at my face. "Clean yourself up!" It was clear the man had lost control and was regretting it.

I ran a trembling finger up to the incision on my tongue. Considering how much it hurt, I was surprised to find that my tongue was still mostly attached. The man walked back to the car and let himself in. He didn't have to say another word, he just stared at me with a venomous glare that dared me to take another step away. I obediently stepped inside and closed the passenger-side door. The low rumble of the idling engine suddenly became much louder. I heard the dirt and gravel kick out from underneath the rear tires as I was pushed back into the seat by the force of the car accelerating.

"Don't be gettin' blood on my upholstery," the man said as he stared straight ahead.

"Thuck you ath-hole," I shot back defiantly as the tears from my eyes ran down and mixed with the blood from my mouth. Nonetheless, I made sure to sop up all the blood with the rag.

The car vibrated as a thick fog enveloped us, and the road that we'd been driving on began to slowly transform from a modern asphalt highway into a rutty byway that I didn't recognize. I got the feeling that wherever we were going, it wasn't a place that was accessible to just any driver.

The car shook as it went over the bumps in front of it. The man didn't slow down. In fact, he sped up, making the ride as uncomfortable as possible for me. Soon, a small building, framed in moonlight and dirty snow, appeared in the distance. As we got closer, I saw gray paint peeling from its clapboard siding. A shabby tin roof covered the structure. The only entrance was a garage door that opened automatically as we approached.

As the car pulled into the structure, I took in my surroundings. This garage was far larger on the inside than it looked on the outside. Grease covered the walls and grimy tools lay haphazardly on the floor. The only light came from a single overhead lamp and a smudgy window that let a little moonlight seep through.

The man pulled inside and revved the engine before killing it. "God damn it!" he yelled as he punched the steering wheel. I didn't know why he was mad. "Don't leave this car," he demanded of me as he stepped out and walked toward a small room that was built into the corner of the garage. The man entered and closed the door behind him.

I did as he had demanded and stayed in my seat, bleeding in silence. Soon the rag became saturated with blood, and I was faced with an undesirable choice—leave the car against the man's instructions or get blood on the seats, also against the man's instructions. I glanced around at the interior of the car, and oddly enough, it was in showroom condition. Hesitantly, I opened the door. It was well greased and moved silently. I stepped outside just as the rag absorbed its last possible drop. The next drop landed on the floor of the garage.

A new voice spoke out to me from the dark. "That looks painful." It had come from just beyond the illuminated area created by the overhead light. "It's okay, you can come closer." The new voice was far less aggressive than the voice of the man who'd cut my tongue.

I waited to let my eyes fully adjust to the conditions, and eventually I was able to make out the shape of a person sitting on the ground. The new person sighed over my reluctance to go to him. "All right, hold on a minute, I'll come to you." I heard the clanging of chains as the form stood up.

A scraping sound, specifically metal being dragged over concrete, filled the room. As he drew nearer to the light, I could see that an automobile engine, attached to him by chains, was being dragged behind him. He huffed as he pulled his burden. The cacophonic sound of clanging links and scraping metal made me cringe. The chains were wrapped around his body and secured with several cast-iron padlocks. This man, a wretch, wasn't going anywhere fast.

"Did he do that to you?" He pointed to my bloody mouth.

"Yeth," I said.

The wretch in front of me laughed. "Well, it looks like he fucked up, then." He pulled closer to me and studied my face. "That's a lot of blood. He ain't allowed to do that to the kids."

We studied each other for a moment. His face was smudged with grease, and he wore blue coveralls. He looked like he might have been about twenty, but they were twenty hard years.

"What'd you do that got him so pissed off?" the wretch asked me. "He usually doesn't make mistakes like that."

I shrugged my shoulders.

"Hmmm, something's got him outta sorts." The wretch stroked the stubble on his face. "What's your name?"

"Tharley Morrithon." The pain and swelling in my tongue made it nearly impossible to speak.

"You said Charley Morrison?"

"Uh huh," I uttered with a nod.

He pondered some more. "The name don't sound important. Where do you live, Charlie?"

"Bilthforth Manthor."

"Ah ha!" he shrieked. "That's it! That's what's got him so outta sorts. He had to go back there."

I stared blankly at the wretch, waiting for an explanation.

"You see, guys like Corbin," he pointed to the office where the man had disappeared, "they don't like visiting places that remind them of when they were alive."

Corbin. The man's name was Corbin. I pondered on whether it was a first name or last name.

The wretch kept babbling. "After the state put him in the hot chair in seventy-four, he became something of a new man. He became a disciple of the Rule Maker."

"Whoth the Rule Makther?"

The poor wretch seemed desperate for friendly conversation. "You know, I've been here ten years, and I haven't totally figured that out for myself. Best I can tell, he's some sort of demon that Corbin pledged his soul to. I don't even know what his real name is. I just call him the Rule Maker because it seems like he lays out all sorts of rules for Corbin to follow. All I know for sure is that he sends Corbin out every Christmas Eve to destroy the lives of certain kids. He sees the same ones over and over. They've got some sort of master plan, but I don't know what it is."

From inside the office, a booming voice spoke out in an inhuman language that sounded to me like chain saws and car crashes. The walls of the garage shook, and my teeth rattled inside my head.

The wretch paused to listen to the voice, then spoke when it was quiet again. "That was the Rule Maker. I ain't ever actually seen him, I only hear him. Anyway, those two really get off on messin' up kids' lives. Just to give you an example of what they do, one kid asked for his parents to go away, so Corbin cut their goddamn heads off. Then, he gave the heads back to the kid the following year, just 'cause the kid said he missed them." The wretch looked around suspiciously to make sure they were still alone. "This shit is planned out, man, and it's totally fucked up."

"Whyth me?"

"Like I said, I don't know how or why he chooses his kids. All I know for sure is that he's not actually supposed to hurt them while they're still young. It's the Rule Maker's number one command. He's just supposed to screw with 'em... take their wishes and twist them around."

More of the booming voice came from the room, and Corbin could be heard arguing back in the same indecipherable language.

"Man, the Rule Maker's pissed," the wretch said with an almost gleeful laugh. "Whatever Corbin had planned for you, it's going to be totally different now. He's going to have to make amends for hurting you."

The voice of the Rule Maker exploded again. For a moment, it felt as if the whole building was going to collapse around me. When it stopped, Corbin yelled back in English, "No, I don't want to give her up! She's my first kil..." He was cut off by a scream from the Rule Maker that was so loud that cracks formed along the dirty window and paint chips fell from the ceiling above.

"Fine! I'll do it!" Corbin shouted in anger and resignation.

The door to the office opened and Corbin backed out slowly. He genuflected as he passed through the doorway. His angry stare began to fade from his face. Turning, he noticed me and the wretch. "Stop talkin' to him before I cut your damn hand off," he said to my new acquaintance.

"Yes, sir!" The wretch snapped up and saluted.

"Get back in the car," Corbin demanded as he threw a clean rag at me.

Not wanting to further upset him, I jumped into the passenger side of the car while the garage door began to open. In the side-view mirror, I could see the wretch lift his arm up and wave goodbye. The car peeled out and sped from the building, clearing the bottom of the door by only a hair. The last I saw of the wretch, he was standing amid a cloud of rubbery smoke looking dejected.

The car tore over a fog enshrouded road while its headlights reflected backwards and created a glowing white aura around it. The engine protested and growled as Corbin shifted into the highest gear. I couldn't see more than five feet out the window, but Corbin only went faster. I looked at the speedometer... 120... 130... 140.

I felt woozy and laid my head back against the headrest and shut my eyes. The pitch of the engine went higher and higher until it faded away completely.

I came to. Had I been unconscious? The night was clear, with no sign of fog. I saw dirty snow banked up along the edges of the road and the car was traveling at a relatively sane speed. We drove for several more minutes in silence until Corbin slammed on the brakes and skidded along the asphalt.

He turned and glowered at me. "Here's the deal, if you can save the girl, you can save yourself."

"What girl?" I asked with the sudden awareness that my mouth no longer hurt. I stuck my tongue out and felt along its side. I could feel a lump of scar tissue, but it was otherwise healed.

"You'll figure out who she is soon enough." He reached over me and opened my door. "You've been given one chance, which I've never given to any kid before. Save her and you'll never see me again. If you don't, I'll be comin' back for you."

I stepped out of the car, confused about my mission. A moment later, the car peeled out and drove off, its rear wheels spitting pebbles at my face. Soon, I was alone. The moonlight reflected off the snow, providing me with at least a little bit of light to take in my surroundings. One of the nearby hills looked familiar, like something I'd seen around my home. I walked that direction and crested it within minutes. From the peak, I found myself looking down on Biltfort Manor, yet something seemed different about it. The cars parked in the manor's roundabout driveway didn't belong to my family—they were older style cars that I didn't recognize. As I trudged through the slushy snow and drew closer, small details came into view that confirmed that something wasn't quite right. The curtains in the windows were the wrong color. Plants and hedges were different, and the Christmas trees, the ones that were all in a magnificent line, seemed to be smaller from when I'd last seen them.

The front door opened, and a well-dressed couple emerged onto the front stoop. The woman, who was holding some neatly wrapped gifts, descended the stairs, followed by the man. They were deep in conversation as they went to one of the cars and opened the trunk.

"Hello?" I shouted to the couple. They both cocked their heads as if they heard something, like I might have been shouting at them from a mile away.

"Did you hear that?" the woman asked the man.

The man shrugged his shoulders. A moment later, a boy, who was maybe a couple of years younger than me, emerged from the front door and ran to the couple. "Shut the door," the man said to the child, "and make sure it's locked." The child ran back up the porch stairs to make sure the house was secured.

"Can you help me?" I asked with uncertainty.

They gave no response, continuing to fret amongst themselves about being late for whatever gathering they were going to. Their conversation was meaningless to me, right up to the point when I heard the woman mention the name Corbin. I froze and listened intently. "… so I put Corbin to work today, mostly some gardening out back, but I also had him dig a hole to plant the Christmas tree."

"Already?" asked the man who I assumed to be her husband. "It's barely Christmas Eve. Why the rush?"

"Have you seen the tree?" she asked. "It's dry. If we wait too much longer there won't be anything left to put in the ground. We won't be breaking fifty-plus years of tradition on my watch."

"Yes," he agreed, "I suppose it's starting to get a little dry." The three of them loaded into the car and drove off without ever acknowledging my presence.

I wasn't sure what to make of the situation, but I decided there would be little to gain by standing around outside. I had a task—a mission, even. I had to push onward. I went to a side door and tried the handle to see if it was unlocked, but I found myself unable to grip it. As I clamped my hand down, the doorknob felt soft, like it was made of dough, and my hand actually sank into its rubbery surface. I gasped and pulled my hand back. Collecting myself, I put my hand out again, this time pushing on the door itself. As before, the door, which should have been rock-solid, felt like dough that my hand could pass through. I put my arm all the way in, then kept pushing. In a few moments, my shoulder was through as well. I took a deep breath and then thrust my leg through. I was half inside and half out, which was an extremely odd sensation. I continued on, pushing my head, and then the rest of my body, into the home. I turned and looked at the door I had just gone through. It was solid as ever.

I explored the house, room to room, with my confusion growing as I saw that all of the furniture and decorations were different from what was supposed to be there. When I got to the kitchen I finally saw it, a wall calendar from 1958. That confirmed a suspicion I'd been having—I was out of my own time.

Not wanting to waste time by pondering my situation, I continued exploring, looking for the "her" who I was supposed to save. I checked every room in the manor, and soon it was clear that nobody was home. As I passed by one of the backrooms, I saw, through the window, a bunkhouse to the rear of the property. It was a small, cozy structure with light emanating from inside. This bunkhouse wasn't something I'd ever seen before—it didn't exist in my time period. I left the manor and headed over to the unfamiliar building.

As I approached, I could see that the bunkhouse was not kept up nearly as well as the manor house. "Hello?" I spoke as I peered into a window. I could see that it was a two-room structure, with the front room doubling as a workshop. In the corner, I could see the back of a man who appeared to be fixing a lawn mower. His shaggy hair fell over his shoulders. In my heart, I already knew who it was, Corbin. I heard the wretch's words sound in my head. *You see, guys like Corbin, they don't like visiting places that remind them of when they were alive.* It was clear that thirty years before my time, Corbin had not only worked as a handyman at Biltfort Manor, but had lived there as well.

My goal was somewhere inside of that bunkhouse, I was sure of it. I entered the same way I'd entered the Manor, by stepping through a closed door. Corbin didn't seem to hear me until he did. The clicking of his ratchet stopped cold as he jerked his head up. "Who's there?" he asked. I stood still. Turning and looking in my direction, he spoke louder, "I said who's there?"

He couldn't see me. I took the opportunity to study his face. He was definitely the same man who'd cut my tongue, but he looked much younger, more vibrant. His face was fuller, and his teeth weren't nearly as nasty.

"What do you want here?" He spoke in my direction, but his gaze fell somewhat to my left.

He fetched a pack of cigarettes from the tabletop next to him and took a moment to light one.

"You're the one who brought me here," I said. He cocked his head, but it was obvious that he couldn't make out what I was saying. I must've sounded like a fly or a gnat to him.

A light thumping sound came from the back room. Corbin instantly decided there was nothing of interest in front of him and shouted behind him, "damn it girl, you best not be makin' noise!" He walked to the bedroom door and kicked it open. Inside, I could see a girl sitting on the floor. She was chained to the bedpost, and she looked miserable in a ratty gray dress and old slippers. I guessed she was probably about twelve or thirteen years old. The girl shivered in fright. It was her, the one I was expected to save.

Corbin reached back and slapped her. "I said shut up!" he screamed as the poor thing winced in pain. Without another word, he walked out, slamming the door shut behind him. By then I had walked into the bedroom—it was just me and her. She waited a minute after he left, then reached under the bed and pulled out a long file. She looked at the door to make sure Corbin wasn't coming back any time soon, then slowly started rubbing the file against one of the links of her chain. She'd already created a large divot, even though the file was dull. She must've been working on it for days. At least the dullness made for quiet work.

The poor girl was filthy and ragged. Black circles ringed her eyes. She paused from her filing and looked up, sensing something in the room with her.

"Hello?" she whispered.

"Can you hear me?" I whispered back.

"Yes, I can hear you. Where are you?"

"I'm right in front of you," I said.

I hadn't meant to scare the girl, but it was understandable when she jumped back in fear. She banged into the bed, pushing it backwards. She shot a fearful look at the door, hoping that Corbin wouldn't come barging back inside. From the other room, the sound of the ratchet turning stopped for what seemed like an eternity, but soon the clicking picked up again.

"I won't hurt you," I told the girl. "What's your name?"

"My name is Magda."

"I'm Charlie," I told her. She reached out her hand to where I was sitting, and I felt its coldness as her fingers passed through my face.

She shivered. "I can feel you!" She managed a small smile.

"What are you doing here?" I asked her.

She told me her story in whispers and gestures. Corbin had purchased her from her father a couple of months earlier, who himself had kept her locked up in a cabin for several years. She recounted some happy memories from her early childhood, when her mother was still alive, but the second half of her existence had been one of misery. As she told it, nobody except her father and Corbin even knew she existed.

For the next hour I was Magda's guest. She was happy to have someone to talk to, even someone she couldn't see. Her years of captivity hadn't broken her spirit, and she talked to me in excited whispers, telling me all of her hopes. I listened, the first person to do so in years, probably. "Do you want to see something secret?" she asked me. I told her yes. She moved to the nearest corner and lifted a small slab of rock from the floor, exposing a hidden compartment within the foundation of the bunkhouse. She reached inside and pulled out her single treasure, a small doll she had created out of various scraps that were left over after Corbin had readied that year's Christmas tree. "This is Perla," she told me as she held the doll up before cradling it like a baby. It was pathetic, made from bits of burlap and sticks tied together with twine. Its head was a small, closed pinecone that was nearly falling off.

"She's beautiful," I told her.

Magda smiled at me. I had gained her trust. "Magda," I asked her, "why don't you let anybody know you're here? Why don't you scream for help?"

"The boy," she said, "he told me he'll kill the boy if I make any noise."

I thought back to the child who'd left with his parents earlier. "He's gone right now. I think they went to a Christmas party."

That seemed to reinvigorate her. She carefully put Perla back into her hiding spot. "You'll be safe here," she said to the doll. She took her seat on the floor and picked up her file, which she began moving back and forth against the chain with determination.

"I'm leaving tonight," she said as she filed. "I'm going to wait for Santa in the big house and have him take me away from here, up to the North Pole where people are nice."

"I don't know if Santa can help you, Magda." Her face fell at those words. "But I can." That made her smile.

Together we came up with a plan. I would try to draw Corbin outside—once he was distracted, Magda would sneak away and run into the manor where she would use the phone to call for the police. "Just dial zero and the operator will connect you," I instructed her. "Don't wait for Santa."

Magda got back to work with her file, and in only a few minutes, she succeeded in cutting through the chain, freeing herself from its bitter grasp.

I moved back into the main room, where Corbin was still working on his lawn mower. Using every last ounce of breath, I yelled his name. "Corbin!" He jerked his head up. "I'm over here!" I yelled.

"The fuck is goin' on here tonight?" His agitation was evident as he stood fully upright. "Who is that?"

"I'm outside!" I shouted as I began pushing myself through the outer wall. He took a step toward the front door, then thought better of it and went to the bedroom. He flung the door open, only to see Magda appear to be sleeping on the floor, still wrapped in her chain.

Leaving the girl where she was, he stomped back across the bunkhouse and shoved open the front door, nearly tearing it off its hinges. His head swiveled both ways as he looked for the source of the distraction.

Moving a little farther outside, I shouted again, "Over here!" I could see Corbin's ears twitch as he tried to understand what he was hearing. He took a tentative step out of the building, but didn't appear willing to move any farther. I screamed for him to come find me. He shuddered momentarily, then a heated sneer grew on his face.

"Whatever son of a bitch is out there, you best run." He pulled a switchblade from his pocket and opened it with a click. He stepped away from the bunkhouse, closer to me. Behind him, I could see Magda slowly stepping out of the bedroom. Her slight frame worked to her advantage as she glided silently across the floor. I kept calling to Corbin, who'd taken about ten steps out of the bunkhouse. It took Magda only a few more seconds until she was standing in the doorway behind him. The sneer dropped from Corbin's face, replaced with a baffled stare as he scratched the back of his head. Magda wavered on the stoop, unsure if she should continue on or not. She began to shake. I was already screaming as loud as I could at Corbin, but it was having less effect with each passing moment.

In desperation I began cussing and swearing. Instantly he turned back and faced my position, as if he could intrinsically tell that someone was cursing his name. The sneer returned to his face, and he boldly stepped closer. Magda took the opportunity and left the bunkhouse, and with feathery footsteps she moved toward the manor. Only a few seconds later, Corbin lost all interest in what I was doing and turned back around, barely missing the sight of Magda disappearing around the corner of the Manor.

I followed her, praying that she'd quickly call the police like we'd planned. I felt a moment of panic when I saw her footprints in the slushy snow, and I knew that we wouldn't have too much time before Corbin came looking for her. Her path led to the opposite side of the Manor, where she had used a rock to break the window into the library. I was impressed with her resolve. I passed through the wall and into the house. I called to her, but got no response. I continued on my way until I made it to the parlor. The Christmas tree was aglow with lights and bulbs and garland. Beautiful gifts were wrapped at its base. Kneeled in front of it was Magda.

"Isn't it beautiful?" she asked as I entered. The blues and reds and greens from the lights colored her face and made her look a little less pathetic.

"C'mon," I insisted, "we need to call the police. The phone is in the kitchen."

Magda looked at the fireplace. "Santa will be here any minute, and he'll save us both!"

"No he won't. Santa's not coming."

"My momma told me all about him. I already made a wish for him to take me away."

I noticed movement in the darkness outside the window. "Magda, we don't have much time."

Emerging from the shadows, I could see Corbin's outline coming toward the house. He was following the path in the snow that had been created minutes earlier by Magda.

"Hurry!" I yelled at her.

Magda shot up, and any fantasies she had about Santa taking her away were momentarily put aside. "What do I do?" she asked in a panic.

"The kitchen! Go to the phone!"

Magda followed my voice as I led her to the kitchen. At that same moment, we heard Corbin kicking in the library glass, making the hole in the window big enough for him to climb through.

Magda found the phone along the wall. "I've never used one before." It was a rotary phone, which I was vaguely familiar with.

"Put your finger in the zero hole and spin the dial.

She did as I told her and put the handset to her face. "I hear it ringing!"

The sound of Corbin stomping around echoed through the halls as he tromped through the house. "Where you at, you little bitch?"

"There's no time!" Magda shrieked as she dropped the handset and ran toward the parlor. The sound of the phone hitting the floor attracted Corbin, who entered the kitchen from the south door as Magda left through the other side.

I followed Magda down the hallway. "Hide!" I shouted to her. "I'll try to distract him!" I ran back toward Corbin and screamed at him, trying to draw him upstairs, but he paid no attention, blasting right past me in his search. I followed him into the parlor where we both scanned the room for Magda. She was hiding.

Without saying a word, Corbin walked up to a set of floor-length curtains that covered one of the large windows. He pushed each one aside with his sinewy arms, but failed to find her. He looked under the table and behind the Christmas tree. Getting annoyed, he tried to coax Magda out. "Now c'mon, girl. Get yourself out here and I won't hurt you."

There was no movement. Corbin scanned the room. Across from him, there was a second set of billowy curtains with a slight bulge in the middle, one that might be hiding a person. He stomped over, pulled his arm back, and punched the bulge square in the middle, only to have his hand connect with something too solid to be human. "Damn it!" he screamed as he shook his hand back and forth in pain. He moved the curtain aside to see what he'd hit, and found a large ceramic Santa that had been placed in the window. He pushed it to the floor in anger and kicked it.

Behind Corbin there was a large set of cabinets. One of the doors moved slightly, revealing Magda's hiding place to me. I knew it wouldn't be long before Corbin checked there.

I yelled to her, "Run now! He's distracted!" She responded immediately, pushing the door open and climbing out from the tight space while Corbin continued his angry tirade on the ceramic Santa, smashing its face with his foot. She ran much faster than her malnourished frame would've suggested—almost fast enough to make it out of the room, but Corbin, who saw her dart away from the corner of his eye, was much faster. He caught up to her right as she passed through the threshold and forcefully yanked her backwards by her hair. She fell to the ground and skidded to the center of the room.

Corbin walked up and kicked her. "Now get over here," he said as he picked her up and slung her over his shoulder. Magda, refusing to give up, bit the back of his arm, drawing blood that ran down her face. He slammed her to the ground in pain, and with his next motion, he withdrew his switchblade and opened it up.

"You don't ever do that!" he yelled at her. "Now stand up."

Magda slowly rose to her feet while Corbin's hand shot out and grabbed her by the throat. He looked right at her. "Bitch." With fury in his eyes, he thrusted his blade deep into her belly. Magda coughed and gasped for breath. Blood oozed from her wound and dripped to the carpet below.

"That's what you get," he said as he let her fall to the ground. A red puddle formed around her dying body.

I kneeled next to her. "I'm here," I told her. "You're not alone."

"I'm glad you're with me," she rasped. Corbin looked at her as if she was insane. I stayed next to Magda as her breaths came with increasingly longer gaps between them. Finally, she breathed no more.

Corbin seemed anxious as he gazed at both the body and the bloody room around him. I could sense that he was trying to figure out a way to erase the mess he'd created, and soon he began nodding his head as if he'd thought of a solution. With little effort, he scooped up Magda's corpse and walked her out of the room. I stayed behind, devastated by what I'd seen.

I soon found that I was immobilized. With my failure, whatever power of movement I'd been granted had ended. Slowly, the room around me began to fade from my vision. One of the last things I remember seeing was Corbin coming back inside and looking at all the blood. He took off his shirt and tried to soak some of it up, but there was no way he could've cleaned it all. He stared at the Christmas tree and felt its dry branches. He left and returned a couple of minutes later with a bottle of clear liquor, which he splashed over the tree and the surrounding floor. The liquor proved its potency when he lit the tree—it flamed up without hesitation. He stepped back from the blaze and watched it grow. The flames crept up the walls and devoured the blood spatters. The pooled blood on the floor began sizzling and smoking under the heat. Corbin left the room, and I heard a car start up. A deep, powerful engine growled out into the night, and soon it faded away.

For my part, I was amid the flames. It was quite a peculiar feeling, as I could feel the heat without any of the accompanying pain that it should've caused. Even in the firelight, my vision continued to grow darker. Soon I could see nothing at all, and I could only hear the sound of the flames lapping their way up the walls of the parlor. Then, I was gone from that place.

It was daylight. I was lying in the snow not too far from the manor. It was immediately evident that I was back in my own time. My father's car was out front, and the parlor, which I had last seen consumed in flames, was intact and proudly displaying our Christmas tree through the window. I got up and stumbled back inside, finding my parents safe in their bed. I vowed that I would put the events of the previous evening out of my mind and enjoy my Christmas, even as I felt the lump of scar tissue on the side of my tongue.

***

By springtime I had mostly succeeded in blocking my memories of Corbin. It helped to find distractions—school, friends— those sort of things helped keep me focused in the present, and made it easier to convince myself that the whole thing had just been one terrible dream. According to the wretch, Corbin visited his charges annually, but I felt that if I could simply forget what happened, then somehow the whole damn thing would simply stop.

Like nearly all of the trees before it, our family's Christmas tree had been firmly planted in the ground, and it was beginning to sprout new needles. The line of trees was now that much longer, and I challenged myself to run the new distance in record time. On a warm day I set my stopwatch and started off on my run. I flew past the teens, twenties, and thirties at a terrific speed, but by the late forties my lungs were burning. "Pace yourself," I thought. I settled into a slower gait while glancing at the stopwatch on my wrist. When I looked up again, I saw her—Magda, standing quietly among the trees. She looked just as I'd last seen her, with her ratty dress and unkempt hair lying stuck against her face. Her skin was gray, almost like she was pulled from a black-and-white TV show. She was trying to speak, but whatever words she was making, they left her mouth silently.

"Hello," I said with cautious surprise. The sight of her made my already racing heart go just a little bit faster. She was a miserable, heartbreaking picture. I felt nothing but pity for her. "It's me, Charlie," I said.

She looked straight up to the sky while her facial features began to warp and distort. Her mouth opened impossibly wide as her forehead and chin melted into her neck, which in turn melted into her torso. I could still see her tongue and her teeth through the large hole that had been her mouth. As she continued to sink into the earth, her whole body turned into black tar, and after a few more moments of me staring in awe, the tar absorbed completely into the earth, leaving a dead spot on the grass.

So much for trying to forget about Christmas. I fell back onto the ground, no longer concerned about setting a new personal record. Images flitted through my mind—I saw Magda in her worn dress, holding onto Perla. I saw Corbin angrily gripping his steering wheel while he sped along his ethereal highway.

Later that day, I walked behind the Manor to the spot where the bunkhouse had once been. It was far enough from the main house that the gardeners felt little need to maintain it full time, and it had reverted to a mostly natural state. I walked among the bushes and sedges that grew there. I had never noticed, but much of the bunkhouse's cement foundation was still in place. It'd been broken up and parts of it had been carried away, but if one knew what to look for, the building's footprint was still visible under a tangle of vines and low-slung branches.

Pushing through the growth, I walked to where the bedroom once was. I scanned the ground, looking for… there it was—the small hole in the foundation where Magda had hidden Perla. It was still covered by a slab of cement. I kneeled down and brushed the dirt from around the slab, then lifted it carefully. A breath of dust escaped from the opening. After a cautious pause, I reached into the darkness. My hand brushed up against a scrap of material, which I grasped and pulled out. I looked at what was in my hands—Perla hadn't aged well, though it was still recognizable as the doll Magda had created. I held it carefully to prevent it from falling apart.

Once I obtained Magda's treasure, I had no real idea of what to do with it. The existence of Perla essentially confirmed that my adventures with Magda and Corbin hadn't been some sort of dream, which set me in a mild panic for the remainder of the day. That night, I ended up storing the doll in the top drawer of my dresser, which is where it stayed—until the next time I saw Magda, that is.

It was probably a couple of months later when her specter showed up in my bedroom. I'd been asleep when a bitter cold wind woke me. I cursed at the open window and pulled the blanket up high to my chin when I saw her. Just like the time before, she was grayish in hue. Moonlight filtered in and lit my room just enough to see her. Her mouth opened and closed, though the only thing I could hear was the rustling of the leaves outside. Slowly, she lifted a finger to my top dresser drawer and pointed.

"What do you want me to do?" I asked her.

She continued pointing at the dresser until little bits of her started falling off. Her finger detached and hit the floor, where it disappeared in a smoky mist. The rest of her arm broke into pieces and followed suit, then her head simply rolled off and hit the ground. It, too, disappeared. The rest of her deteriorated in the same manner. Soon, there was nothing left.

I took to carrying Perla in my pocket wherever I went. It was bulky and uncomfortable, but it seemed like Magda had gone out of her way to send a message to me, though I wasn't sure exactly what it was. Still, I felt that it would be wise to keep Perla close.

Many times I contemplated telling my mother and father about what'd happened. They were very devoted parents, but I had the fundamental understanding that there was really nothing they could do for me, even if they had believed my story, which they wouldn't have. However, I did have an interesting conversation with my father about the missing 1958 Christmas tree. He had been in town talking with some long-time residents, and they told him that nearly half the manor had burned down at some point during the fifties. "The fire started with the Christmas tree, apparently," he explained to me. He glanced around the parlor, where we were sitting. "They did a marvelous job matching the new construction to the old," he said. I agreed with him. "So, it looks like that's your answer about the missing tree. It got destroyed before they ever had a chance to put it in the ground. I'm guessing that they left a gap there as a memorial to the lost tree, kind of like a gloomy placeholder for the Christmas that wasn't," he surmised.

"Yeah, I know," I said quietly.

After school started in the fall, I would often stop by the library on my way home to look through the old microfiches of the local newspapers, hoping to find a mention of Magda. I had no luck. It was almost like she never existed. I did find information on Corbin—his last name was Montreau, and just like the wretch had told me, he'd been put to death in the electric chair in 1974 after being convicted for a string of murders dating from 1960. The police and prosecutors never even knew about Magda, his first victim.

More months passed. I didn't see Magda in that intervening time, though I could feel her presence around me. My unease grew as Christmas drew nearer and my memories of Corbin came into sharper focus. I threw myself into my schoolwork and chores, trying my best to keep occupied.

On December 24th I went to church with my parents. I prayed for salvation, forgiveness, and everything in-between. I wasn't sure if it would help, but I knew it wouldn't hurt. My parents let me open a couple of gifts before they went to sleep, but the rest were saved for Christmas itself. I made sure to cherish the moment, not really knowing what fate awaited me and my family that night.

My parents went to sleep early, but they let me stay up. "Not too late," my father warned. "Santa won't stop here if you're still awake when he passes by." He winked while I forced a laugh.

The house became eerily quiet. I sat in the parlor next to our grand, decorated tree. The fireplace kept me warm as I settled into my father's leather chair. The old manor creaked and groaned as the night cooled. I grabbed a blanket off the couch and pulled it up to my chin. I waited in silence. I might have dozed off, so I'm not sure what time it was when I heard the low rumbling of an engine. I perked my head up. *It's really happening,* I thought. The sound grew louder as its source drew closer. The headlights illuminated the room and cast morbid looking shadows along the wall. The car came to a stop right outside the parlor window, but the engine kept going. It revved until the walls shook from the noise.

I completely lost my nerve at that point. I'd sworn to myself that I would meet Corbin head-on, but in that moment, listening to the engine scream, I threw my blanket off and ran upstairs to my parents' bedroom.

I got to their door and slammed into it as I turned the knob. It might as well have been a block wall—it didn't budge. No matter how hard I tried, it wouldn't open. Outside, I could hear Corbin kill the engine. The complete silence that followed was broken by the car door opening and then closing, followed by gravelly footsteps coming up to the house.

I could hear nothing from the other side of my parents' door. I said a prayer that they were okay and then walked down the hallway toward the stairs. I poked my head over the banister and stared down. Some firelight from the parlor flickered beneath me, but for the most part I was looking straight into darkness.

Corbin's voice fractured the still air. "You can come down now."

I waited at the top of the stairs.

"Don't piss me off again, boy. I'm in the kitchen."

I walked down the stairs with wobbly legs that could barely support me. I felt like I weighed a thousand pounds.

He was in the kitchen going through our refrigerator. "You didn't leave out any milk and cookies," he said with a wicked laugh. He came out from behind the refrigerator door holding a turkey leg, which he pointed in the direction of the table. "Sit down," he said right before taking a bite. In his other hand he had a gallon of milk, which he took a swig from as soon as he swallowed his first bite of turkey.

We both sat at the table, directly across from one another.

"So you failed, kid." He took another bite of turkey before speaking again. "You had a chance to save Mary and you wasted it. You changed virtually nothin' that happened that night… almost like you weren't there at all. She died the same way."

"Her name's Magda," I corrected.

"It don't matter much. It certainly don't change the fact that she's a dead little bitch."

I tried to stare him down, but I was shaking too much to maintain eye contact. Instead, my gaze shifted to the floor.

Corbin glanced around the room. "Never cared for this house much." He put the milk bottle to his lips and drank the whole thing, nearly an entire gallon. He belched loudly and spoke again.

"I don't like this place at all. I don't like being here, and I certainly don't like you. The problem is, I don't choose who calls out to me. Either I hear your thoughts, or I don't. And if I hear you, you're basically fucked."

Corbin dropped the turkey leg to the floor and pulled a cigarette out of his shirt pocket. A flame came from his finger and lit it. He took a long drag and continued. "I don't fancy coming back here year after year, but as long as you're alive I gotta do it. You see, I can't physically hurt a kid I visit, at least not while he's still young, but I can kill his family, I can kill his friends—heck, I can even kill his dog and take all of his favorite little things. Year after year, I come back, each time taking a little more. I think my buddy at the garage might've explained it to you." He stared across the table at me until I could feel his glare penetrate to the back of my skull. "I'm gonna make you a deal. We can just end it this year."

"How do we do that?" I thought.

"You ask for your protection to be removed." He said it slowly and seriously, before perking up and speaking again. "So that's it, you ask for it, and then I gut you like a little piggy, and the rest of your family stays safe."

"I don't want to be gutted like a pig."

"Of course you don't. Nobody does. That's what makes it so goddamn fun. But I'll tell you what, if you don't agree to this, I'll make sure that you wish you had." He pointed upstairs to my parents' bedroom. "Remember when you wished that you could beat your father at basketball?"

I thought back to months earlier when my father and I had gone to the park and played one-on-one. I'd made such a wish after he'd defeated me handily. I guess I'd reached the age where he no longer felt he was required to let me win.

Corbin let the memory sink in, then started up. "Well, you won't have any trouble beating your father after I rip his fucking arms off. And remember when you wished for a little brother or sister?"

I nodded yes.

"Good, I'm glad you remember. Let's just say I'll take care of that too. Only, it won't be your daddy makin' the deposit." He glared at me. "And that's just the beginning. They'll wind up dead, sooner or later, as will everyone you know or care about, that is, after I've had my fun with them."

Okay, just kill me, I thought.

"No, you have to say it out loud."

"Kill m-," I trailed off, unable to say it completely.

"Say it!" he screamed.

"Kill me!" I finally blurted out with tears beginning to flow down my cheeks.

He relaxed back into his chair and took a drag from his cigarette. "Well?" he said.

I didn't know what he wanted.

"At least try to make this interesting for me. I already made the trip out here." He took another drag of his cigarette and flicked it to the ground. "You stupid? Run."

I stood up and slowly backed out of the kitchen. Corbin went back to the refrigerator and began rooting around. "Run," he said with his head hidden behind the refrigerator door.

I took his advice and darted through the kitchen doorway and down the hallway. I paused to consider which way I should go. My gut instinct told me upstairs, but as my foot hit the first step I saw her—Magda, standing silently before me. Her arm rose up, and she pointed her finger in the direction of the front door. I quickly decided that hiding in the nearby woods would be best. I shot out the front entrance and down the steps.

As I turned and headed toward the wooded area at the edge of the property, I heard a crashing of glass behind me. I twisted around and saw the refrigerator, which had been thrown through the kitchen window, smashing to the ground. Corbin poked out from the shattered window and laughed. "There wasn't anything good to eat in there anyway." He effortlessly hopped out the window and landed on the ground.

I doubled my pace, running over the lawn to the wood-line at the edge of the property. Once under the cover of the trees I slowed down to catch my breath. I looked back, but I couldn't see my tormentor until I heard a rustling in the tree above me. Looking up, I saw a smiling Corbin standing on one of its branches. I took off running again, farther and farther away from the house, for what seemed to be an eternal uphill sprint.

I fell down exhausted. The cold night air was torturing my lungs, and I was beginning to think that any effort to escape was probably futile. As I lay panting on the ground, I saw Magda once again. Her mouth was opening and closing, and like the time before, her finger rose up and pointed. I brushed myself off and looked to where she was directing me. It was back from where I'd come. "I just came from there," I protested.

Then, with a high-pitched shriek, her voice broke through, "Save ussssss!"

I looked again at where she was pointing. Her finger wasn't aimed at the manor house like I had originally thought, it was aimed at the row of Christmas trees that were well on the other side of the property.

I started running again, making my way to where she'd directed me. Corbin's voice boomed from behind. "Getting tired yet?" He gave a frenzied laugh that resonated through the woods.

I ran as hard as I could until I tasted bile coming up from my throat. For all my effort, Corbin was never far from me, taunting me and laughing. My eyes filled with tears, dirt and sweat, making it nearly impossible to see where I was going. I tried to wipe them clean with my sleeve, but that only rubbed the dirt in.

Magda's shrill scream howled out once again. "Charlie!" I stumbled toward the direction of the voice and finally collapsed in despair.

The sound of crunching snow told me my pursuer was closing in. In a final act of desperation, I had the thought that maybe Perla could be used as some sort of protective talisman. I grabbed the doll from my pocket and held it up in front of me as Corbin approached, but I lost all hope when I saw Perla begin to fall apart in my hands. Corbin just looked at me and laughed. "You think a fuckin' doll is gonna help you?" He kept stepping toward me unabated. The doll was worthless.

His arm shot out and he grabbed my shirt, using it to lift me from the ground. "You're a pathetic little shit," he said as I heard his switchblade open. My sight grew dimmer until I only saw darkness. "It's time for you to die." I faded out of consciousness and my body went limp.

***

"Okay, so then what happened?" my son asked in anticipation. I was telling him the same story I just told you, though for him I cleaned it up a bit.

"Well, I'm not sure exactly," I responded.

"What do you mean you're not sure? Where did that man Corbin go?"

I looked at my son's face, which was lit by the few remnants of dusky sunlight that filtered through the window of my study. I could see his brow furrow as he tried to make sense of what he'd just heard. He was just about the same age as I was when Corbin first came to me. He looked out the window to the grounds of Biltfort Manor. Our second-floor vantage point gave us a spectacular view.

"I don't know where he went exactly. I guess he returned to his garage. All I know for sure is that I woke up the next morning in the same spot where he left me. I brushed off the snow and dirt and crawled back to the house. I never saw him or Magda again."

"And grandma and grandpa were okay?"

"Yeah, they were fine." My parents, who'd lived happy lives, passed away naturally many years later. They were never even aware of what had happened.

"Why didn't he kill you?"

"I'm not really sure." I continued to study my son's face to gauge his reaction to what I was telling him. I didn't want him to get too disturbed by what he was hearing. I suppose it may seem weird that I was telling my young son a real-life horror story, on Christmas Eve of all nights, but I had some good reasons. First, it was therapeutic to finally tell someone what'd happened all those years ago. He was at the right age where he'd still believe me, but was old enough to rationalize it away if he wanted to. Second, I wanted to make sure that Corbin hadn't ever come to visit him, and judging by how he responded to what I was telling him, he'd never met the man. Finally, I told him the story because he asked me about the 1958 Christmas tree. And to be clear, my son didn't ask me why it was missing, as I had once asked, instead he asked why it was so big.

I continued with my story. "So that spot where I woke up Christmas morning, the spot that Magda lured me to, can you guess where it was?"

"It was where the 1958 tree is. Right?"

"Yep!" I said. "When I passed out, I dropped Perla in that exact spot. And do you remember what she was made out of?"

The cogs and wheels in his brain turned. "Wasn't her head a pinecone?"

I nodded yes. "That next spring, I noticed a new tree growing. By the time the next Christmas came along, it was already over ten feet tall.

My son, who was much more logical than I ever was, took issue. "Trees don't grow that fast! And you didn't even plant it correctly, you just dropped a thirty-year-old pinecone in the snow!"

"I know all that," I said in agreement. "I can't totally explain it. All I know for sure is that the tree kept growing at a tremendous rate. After a few years, it was as big as the trees that had been there for decades. Now, it's the biggest tree out of all of them, by far."

My son scratched his head in contemplation as he looked out the large picture window. The fading sunlight painted the snowy ground gold and silhouetted the Christmas trees against the sky. The fireplace behind us crackled as the festive lights along the eaves turned on automatically, illuminating the house. "I bet Magda's buried under that tree," he concluded.

I was speechless. What's the expression? Out of the mouths of babes? He was right. Sometimes the truth is so obvious that you can't help but miss it if you're looking too close. You never see the full picture if you spend all your time looking at the individual brush strokes, but all of the sudden, everything made perfect sense. I was almost embarrassed at the fact that I never figured it out for myself. Corbin, after murdering Magda, needed a place to quickly dispose of her body, and what better place than a hole that he'd already started digging and would no longer be needing?

"Dad?" my son prodded, bringing me out of my deep thought.

"I think you're right, son."

"Whoa," he said in awe.

For thirty years I'd believed I'd failed Magda, but I finally realized that when I dropped Perla in that exact spot, I'd actually given her spirit the means to make her mark on the world. She was the girl who nobody knew existed—the girl whose entire life was erased without leaving even the slightest mark behind. The tree served as a living grave-marker that was grander than anything that could be carved from stone. It was a way for her to be remembered, a way for her to avoid being removed from history completely. The entire time, her spirit had been pushing that tree up towards the heavens, that's why it was so big. I never saved her life, but whatever it was that I managed to do, I somehow saved her soul. I can't say that I completely understand how it worked out this way, but I know in my heart that I'm right.

"Should we have her moved to a cemetery?" my son asked, again breaking me out of my thought.

"No, I think she's happy where she is." I put my hand on his shoulder as we both stared out at Magda's tree. "You know what? I don't think my job is done. We have some time before your mom gets home. Do you want to go down there and put a few ornaments on that tree?"

"We'll have to bring a ladder," my son replied with a serious tone, "but we should do it. Magda will like that, I think."

"She will. I'm sure of it. And next year," I said, "we'll hire a crane to decorate the whole thing with thousands of lights. We'll make it a new tradition. It will be the grandest Christmas tree in the state, maybe even the world."

"Cool!" he said, barely containing his excitement.

On our way out of the house we stopped by the parlor, where my son pulled an armload of ornaments off of our tree. I took only one, a little figurine of Santa, and with that, we headed outside to spread some long overdue Christmas cheer.

THE GRIM MELODY

Brady Hollis fell forty-seven floors and lived.

Even after hitting the ground he was still conscious. He was aware of the screams and the panic that surrounded him, and he felt a tinge of relief when the ambulance and firetruck arrived. There was no pain when the responders carefully placed him on a backboard and finally got him into the ambulance.

"Inbound with a male construction worker. Twenty-seven years," the paramedic said into his radio as she called ahead to the hospital. She looked Brady up and down. "Possible blunt force trauma. Pulse sixty, blood pressure one-twenty over eighty."

The driver raised his eyes and shot a look through the rear-view mirror. "Double check that. There's no way his vitals are THAT normal."

"I already did!" the tending paramedic shot back.

Their trip was short—Saint Augustus Hospital was only a few blocks away and the midday traffic was light. As they pulled up outside the ER, the ambulance doors were flung open and Brady, still alert, was greeted by a team of medical professionals who tended to him immediately.

"He fell from the top of that huge tower they're building," the paramedic reported.

The doctor flashed a light into Brady's eye. "How is he still in one piece?"

Both paramedics looked at each other and shrugged as Brady was wheeled into the emergency room. "I don't know. When we got there, he was on the street. Witnesses said he hit the asphalt head on."

"Wow. Well, let's take a look at him," the doctor said as he followed the gurney inside.

The stunned doctors kept him overnight for observation, but aside from some bruising and abrasions, they found nothing wrong with him. His construction buddies visited—more than could fit in the room—and eventually they had to be shooed out by Carla, Brady's nurse for the night. "He needs room to breathe, gentleman," she said as she worked her way past the broad-shouldered men.

The men said their goodbyes with a procession of handshakes, fist bumps, and solid pats on the shoulder. Soon the room quieted down, and Carla was alone with Brady. She went through her spiel—call button on the side of the bed, pitcher of water on the table, TV remote next to the bedrail—but halfway through she stopped her automated speech and looked at him in awe. "I'm sorry, but did you really fall from the top of that building? It's just so hard to believe."

"Yeah. I was guiding a beam into place." Brady closed his eyes as he tried to recall. "I unhooked my lanyard, just for a moment. I was trying to step around a support column. And then, I'm not sure what happened. Somehow I slipped."

"Incredible," Carla said. "Just incredible. You must be made of titanium." Brady only smiled in response. With that, Carla encouraged her patient to get some sleep and made her way from the room.

Soon, the activity in the hospital died down, and only the murmuring of the nurses and the occasional beeping of a machine could be heard in the rooms. Brady began to rest. His eyes had been closed for no more than five minutes when a gruff voice, speaking too softly to be understood, sounded out from within his room.

Brady shot up and looked around. "Who's there?" he questioned into the darkness. Before he could reach for the dimmer to turn the lights up, a small child-like form quickly jumped onto his bed.

Brady was immobilized, whether it was from fear or from an unseen force, he didn't know. He could sense the intruder staring at his face. "What's going on?" he asked with a shaky voice.

The intruder sat atop Brady's chest, his finger poking Brady's forehead. "You've been given life," the gruff, gravelly voice said. "Go live it. Be happy. Be sad." With that, the small form jumped from the bed and scuttled out of the room.

Brady, finding his freedom of movement restored, hit the call button.

"Nursing station—can I help you?"

"There was someone… something in my room." Brady's voice was shaking from the experience.

"I'll have Carla check in on you. Give me just a minute."

Brady actually waited less than a minute before Carla came through his door. She scanned the room for any sign of an unwelcome guest. "Was there someone in here with you?"

Brady pondered on what had just happened. "Yeah, a little man maybe?" All he'd seen was a small silhouette. "Actually, I don't know what it was. It was the size of a kid, but it moved way too fast and, really, I just don't know."

Carla looked him over and studied his breathing pattern. "You suffered quite a trauma today. I'll call the doctor and maybe he'll let me give you something to help you sleep."

Brady shook his head. "No, it's okay. Whatever it was, it's gone now."

The brunette nurse looked around. "Yeah, we're alone. But I have to tell you, I was just down the hall, and I didn't see anyone come out of your room."

"I understand," Brady said, still a little shaky. "Maybe I just imagined it."

Carla studied her patient, and even though his blood pressure and heart rate were normal on the monitors, he appeared sweaty and disheveled. She reached for his pillow and fluffed it up. "Well, you're never going to get to sleep if we can't calm you down," she said as she replaced the pillow.

"I'll be fine," he said.

"Of course you'll be fine," she replied with a smile. "You have me for your nurse. Would some soft music help you relax?"

"Sure. Maybe something classical."

"Perfect," she said as she fiddled with the TV remote. "There's a channel on here that plays nothing but classical."

Brady listened as the pleasant notes filled the room. "Thank you," he said, beginning to relax. "Almost as good as playing it myself."

"Oh, you play?"

"Yes, piano. Mostly when I'm stressed."

Carla glanced at the construction worker's beefy fingers and imagined them working their way across a set of piano keys.

Brady noticed her expression. "Silly, I know."

"Not silly at all," she said. "I wish we had one here for you to play, but since we don't, just try your best to relax."

Brady looked into her pretty brown eyes. "I think I'll be okay. I feel better already."

She smiled at him and pointed to the call button. "I'm here until seven in the morning. Let me know if you need anything."

He couldn't help but smile as she sauntered away.

****

From that point on, Brady Hollis lived a charmed life. His construction firm paid out a large settlement rather than risk going to court over the accident. The strange thing was, Brady never even threatened to sue them. As he saw it, he was the one at fault—he knew better than to remove his lanyard. But the lawyers, being lawyers, wanted to make sure the company had no further liabilities, and they insisted he take the money.

He left the construction industry and found work as an assistant to a veterinarian. He made far less money, but with his settlement that wasn't really a concern. Working for the vet was a far more rewarding experience than guiding girders into place. And for whatever reason, he kept running into Carla. First, he saw her at the supermarket where they said an awkward hello. A few weeks later, she brought her Chocolate Lab to the vet for a checkup and was surprised to find Brady working there. He saw her again at the car wash, a concert, and the dentist. He finally took it as a sign from above and asked her out on a date. She accepted.

The date went well, as did every date after that. They married after six months. Brady didn't think he could be any happier, until the birth of his daughter.

Brady lived a charmed life, indeed. And just when everything was perfect, that's when he saw the little man again.

Lying in bed half asleep, Brady watched the light from the television flicker through the bedroom. Carla slept peacefully next to him. On his nightstand, a baby monitor played the sounds from the nursery where Charlotte, his nine-month-old daughter, slept. His eyes closed, sleep almost taking hold for the night.

A gruff voice came through the monitor, speaking some sort of foreign language. Brady shot up and looked at the device on the nightstand. Again the rough-edged voice came through, almost beckoning him to the room. In only seconds, Brady darted from the bed and down the hallway. As he flung the door to the nursery open, a horrific sight greeted him—his daughter was in the arms of what could best be described as a half-size adult. Tufts of gray hair poked out from underneath a bowler hat. His cracked, weathered skin was stretched tautly across his face. A dark, dusty suit covered his body. In his hand was a large knife.

"Get the hell away from her!" Brady screamed as he moved into the room. "Carla!" he shouted behind him, "Call 911!"

The little man hissed at Brady as he moved the knife up to the throat of the little baby. Brady stopped dead. His daughter, who looked to be yet unharmed, surveyed the room curiously, seemingly unaware of the danger she was in.

Neither man moved as the lights from the mobile zipped across the room. "Just put her down, please," Brady said. He could barely hear himself over the beating of his heart.

The little man smiled, and Brady could swear dust spewed out from the cracks on the man's lips. With no warning, the little man jumped across the room in a single leap with the baby still cradled in his arms. He hopped up to the windowsill and kicked the glass out. The whole thing happened before Brady could even react, and he watched in horror as the little man leapt through the shattered opening.

Carla came screaming down the hall holding her cell phone. "What's happening?" she demanded.

"Did you call 911?" Brady yelled over his shoulder as he ran to the window.

"Yes! What's going on?"

"Stay here!" he ordered as he jumped out the second-floor window. He landed on an awning and then rolled off to the ground below. Despite some scrapes and scratches, he was unhurt. He had no idea where the little man had run off to, and resorted to screaming the name of his daughter as if she could answer. Lights in the neighbors' houses came on. From far away, he could hear the sound of police sirens.

He picked a direction and ran, hoping he was headed the right way. As he got to the end of the street, he heard the loud cry of his daughter break through the night air. Alive! He ran toward the crying and found her pushed under a juniper bush. He carefully picked her up, and to his great relief, found no injuries. The little man was gone. He arrived back at the house at the same time the police arrived. With tears in his eyes, he handed her to Carla, then fell to the ground shaking.

The next few hours blurred into each other. Carla took the baby, along with a police escort, to get checked out at the hospital. Brady stayed behind and gave his witness statement to a million different officers. As the police were finishing up, he got a text from Carla—*Charlotte okay, no injuries. Almost done. Be home soon. Love You.*

He thanked the officers for their help, and for agreeing to keep a unit parked out on the street until morning. He retreated inside and waited. When the house became too quiet for him, he went to the closet and did something he hadn't done in a couple of years. He retrieved a keyboard piano, laid it across the bed, and plugged it in. It was a nice model, a fancy one that Carla had bought for him right after they were married. He'd only touched it a few times, but at that moment, he needed its calming power more than ever.

For Brady, it was like the return of an old friend, and he kept playing right up until the moment when Carla returned. She entered with Charlotte, and he held them both. They laid Charlotte down on their bed where she slept peacefully.

Carla glanced at the keyboard. "I thought you forgot about that thing," she said in a low voice.

Brady shook his head. "Of course not."

"Play something relaxing."

Brady lowered the volume as not to wake Charlotte, then began moving his fingers from key to key.

Carla closed her eyes and listened. "What's it called?" she asked as the notes floated through her mind.

"It's a sonata."

"Yeah, but what's its name?"

"I haven't given it a name yet." Brady kept playing the soothing melody.

"You wrote this?"

"A long time ago, yes. It's actually unfinished."

Carla kept listening. "It sounds finished to me."

"This is just the first movement. It still needs two more."

"Well, it's beautiful already." Carla snuggled up to Charlotte at the top of the bed and closed her eyes. "Keep playing," she requested.

Brady did as he was asked. Even after Carla fell asleep he kept going, and he managed to come up with the backbone for the second movement of his sonata by the morning.

The next day they installed a top-of-the-line security system—cameras, sensors, alarms, live monitoring—everything that the security company offered. They had new doors and windows installed, too. Their house became a fortress, and Brady and Carla felt safe.

***

For the next five years, Brady had no worries. The little man faded from his daily thoughts, but not from his memories. In the meantime, they had a son who they named Carl. He had Brady's eyes and his laid-back nature. Brady was fiercely devoted to his family, and lived to make sure they had everything they needed.

On a mundane day, Carla decided to take the children and visit her mother. Brady, who had plenty of yard work to keep him occupied, decided to stay home. He helped her load the children into their car seats and kissed them all goodbye.

He watched as the minivan backed out of the driveway and moved slowly down the street. As he waved goodbye, a movement in the vehicle's cargo area caught his attention. He squinted to get a better look, and saw, waving at him, the little man. His face was pressed right up against the window.

Brady took off after the van, but couldn't keep up. He waved his arms frantically to flag down Carla, but neither she nor the children seemed to notice. As they turned the corner, Brady could still see the little man waving and smiling. He stuck his tongue out at Brady and licked the window.

Fumbling through his pockets, Brady searched desperately for his cell phone. His first call was to Carla, but it went straight to her voicemail. He called 911 next and screamed at the operator for help. The police responded quickly and arrived to find Brady furiously pounding his fingers on his cell phone screen, trying to get a call through to his wife.

Hours went by with no sign of his family. As had happened years earlier, he answered a million questions from the officers. One of them gave him a look of pity, while others stared at him suspiciously.

A day went by—a whole damn day—without Brady hearing from his family. The police were "looking" for them, he was assured, though it was clear they seemed to think it was a domestic squabble playing out rather than some sort of crime. Brady's description of the little man hiding in the back of the van didn't seem to hold much weight. He himself had spent the night combing the city, checking every possible route between his house and his mother-in-law's. Family members and friends joined in too, though nobody could seem to find them.

The next afternoon, he got a call from a neighbor who was among the searchers looking for his family. "Hello?" Brady said anxiously into his phone.

"Hey Brady, it's William, I think I found your van."

"Where? Where is it?!" Brady shot up from his seat.

"I was passing over Cooper's Bridge, and I saw it off the road, down by the river. I'm pretty sure it's yours."

"Are they in there?" Brady grabbed his keys and ran to his car.

"I'm heading down there right now." He could hear William panting as he climbed his way from the road and down the embankment. "Yeah, it's definitely your van. Give me just a minute, it's still far away."

Brady stopped short of his car, his keys still in his hand. He waited, still as a statue. He could hear the gravel crunch under William's steps as he made his way nearer to the car, then there was a moment of silence.

"William!" Brady shouted. "What do you see?"

"Uh…" It seemed like William didn't want to speak.

"What do you see?"

"They're in there. All three of them." Brady breathed out a short breath. "The door is locked. They're… they're not moving."

Through the phone, he could hear William rapping his fist against the window of the minivan. "Carla! Are you okay?" Just silence. Then again, "Carla! Can you hear me?"

The phone dropped from Brady's hand and clattered to the driveway, but he could still hear William's desperate voice. "Carla! Carla!"

Having reached his darkest moment, Brady melted to the ground. Lying on his back, he stared straight into the cloudless blue sky. "Kill me," he said.

There was an abrupt change in the pitch of William's voice. "Carla? Are you okay?" Brady lifted his head up. The faint, muffled sound of a female voice could be heard in response, then William spoke again. "Brady, I think she's okay. Carla, open the door."

Brady sat up and grabbed the phone. Putting it next to his ear, he could hear the unmistakable sound of the car door clicking open and then the sound of one—no, two—two children as they began crying. They were alive, all of them. He looked to the sky. "Thank you," he whispered.

That night, after endless rounds of police questioning, Brady found himself unable to sleep. Carla and the children, who had no recollection of what happened, dozed peacefully. He went to the closet where his dusty keyboard sat and retrieved it with jittery hands. As soon as it was within his grasp he felt reassured, as if everything was instantly better. He played.

****

Brady and Carla's first grandchild was beautiful. She had a shockingly full head of hair and the cutest button nose that he'd ever seen. She seemed to most resemble her mother, Charlotte.

Brady, who had spent thirty rewarding years working at the same veterinary clinic, found himself with plenty of extra time when he retired. He was able to offer Charlotte one of the most valuable gifts a new parent can receive—free babysitting.

It was with that offer that he found himself at his daughter's house two days a week, babysitting the granddaughter he was so proud of. As the little one approached eight months, she began scooting around on the floor like a little army ranger. Brady followed her around the home, smiling at her delightful little movements as she made her way across the living room.

THUMP

Brady tilted his head at the sound that had come from upstairs. He was sure nobody else was in the home. *Probably nothing,* he thought as he resumed following the baby.

THUMP

That one was louder. After a moment's pause, he scooped up the baby and went up the stairs to investigate.

THUMP

It was coming from the nursery. He pushed the door open and looked inside. The baby cooed in his hands as he took a sweeping look around the quiet room. Just as he was about to turn and leave, he noticed some movement in the crib. Whatever it was, it was covered by a blanket, and it had just rolled over.

Brady stepped closer to the crib with his free arm outstretched. He wondered if Charlotte had gotten a cat and not mentioned it to him. He reached into the crib hesitantly, as if he knew something was really wrong. He moved the blanket aside and saw, sleeping peacefully in the crib, the same granddaughter that he believed he was already holding.

His gaze shot over to the little body in the crook of his arm. It was much bigger than the baby he'd been holding just a few moments earlier, more like the size of a small child, and it was dressed in a dusty gray suit.

Brady dropped the gray bundle to the floor and watched in revulsion as it rolled over and scuttled out of the nursery.

"What are you?" Brady shouted out to the hallway. He looked behind him to make sure his granddaughter was okay in the crib, but it was empty.

In a panic, Brady looked all around the room for his granddaughter. It was a pointless search that yielded only further dread when he couldn't find her anywhere.

He ran out of the bedroom and down the hallway. Hearing a commotion from the kitchen, he descended the stairway three steps at a time and ran to the source of the noise. He immediately saw that the oven was on, though it had been off earlier. He jumped across the room in one bound and nearly took the oven door off in his haste to open it.

Inside, his little baby granddaughter turned her head and looked at him, unharmed in the still-cool oven. He pulled her out and held her closely.

After checking the baby to make sure she was unharmed, he debated whether or not he should call the police, but he intrinsically knew that the little man wouldn't be found, and that his story would make no sense to anyone. Instead, he walked carefully to the couch and comforted her. He willed his arms to stop trembling, though he knew there was only one thing that would truly calm him. His fingers twitched in anticipation of going home and playing his keyboard.

****

Brady was in his hospital bed, staring up at the ceiling. Around him, machines beeped and whirred. And even though he could no longer communicate, he was aware of what was going on around him.

"He could go at any time," the doctor advised his family. "Stay nearby." Everyone was there, everyone he loved, anyway. Next to him sat his granddaughter, the same one who'd been saved from the oven twenty-five years earlier. She held onto his hand tenderly. The rest of his family, through their teary eyes, assured one another that he'd lived a great life, and that he was moving on to his next great adventure, whatever that might be.

Brady smiled inwardly and agreed with them. *Don't be sad for me. I wouldn't change a damn thing,* he thought.

The machine beeped.

No, not a damn thing.

The machine stopped beeping.

Brady smiled as his lungs expelled their last bit of air. Then, the oddest thing of all happened to him—he didn't die. He was still lying in his bed, fully aware of his surroundings, as the doctor came and listened for his heartbeat.

"He's passed," the doctor said solemnly.

But that's not true, Brady thought as he witnessed his family comfort one another. His eyes darted around the room in confusion. *I'm still here.* His body remained breathless. A movement in the corner of the room caught his eye, and there he saw the little man, standing with his arms folded across his chest. Despite the fact that they'd had several close encounters over his lifetime, Brady had never gotten the chance to really stare at him. And now that he could see him clearly, he thought that the little man looked like a breathing corpse.

The color left Brady's vision, like a television flickering into black and white. His family became as still as statues and there was no more sobbing, no more comforting. He observed the little man walk from the room.

Cautiously, Brady sat up. "Carla?" he said to his wife. She remained motionless. He pulled the medical devices and monitors from his body and stepped down from the bed. From outside of his hospital room he could hear croaky mutterings, almost sounding like an invitation to follow. He took an uncertain step toward the door and found that he could walk without difficulty. He took one last look back at his family and then left the room.

The hospital was abandoned. Its silent hallways seemed to pulse with gray light that bathed the dingy walls. Around the corner is where he found the little man, standing in the middle of the corridor. Oddly, Brady felt no fear of the menacing person who'd popped up throughout his life. "Who are you?" he asked.

"Hollings," the little man answered.

"Am I dead?"

"Still alive," the little man responded. "Still falling."

"Still falling? From where?"

"From the building."

Brady shook his head. "That's not possible. That was over sixty years ago."

"No. Only two seconds."

The weight of the little man's words pulled Brady to the floor, where he sat on the cold tile. "I'm imagining all this? This is all in my mind?"

"Nearly a whole life. Compressed. By me."

"Carla, the kids, they were never real?"

With a furrowed brow, the little man thought through his response. "In a billion years the world will be a barren rock. Who will be left to say what was genuine and what wasn't?"

Brady shook his head. "I don't know."

Suddenly, Brady was no longer standing in a hallway, but a large room that was so dimly lit that he couldn't see to the walls. A spotlight lit up a corner, and Brady saw a piano illuminated in the circle of light.

"Almost done. Finish your sonata," the little man croaked.

"That's what this is all about? A song?"

"Yes."

Brady stood up and walked over to the piano. He looked down at his fingers, which were no longer gnarled with age, but resembled the vigorous hands of his construction worker days.

Anticipation—waiting—the little man watched eagerly. "I heard you play the first movement yesterday. Most beautiful song. When I realized you were going to die, I wanted to give you a chance to finish."

"But you terrorized me…"

"When did you write? Only when you were scared or upset. I had to encourage you, from time to time."

Brady thought back to all the times when Hollings had terrorized him. It was after Charlotte had been kidnapped that he worked on his second movement. And when Carla and the kids disappeared for a day—after he got them back, he spent the next two sleepless nights composing most of the third movement. He slowly began to understand what the little man was telling him. After the incident with his granddaughter in the oven, he nearly finished the song, going back and filling in all the blank spaces he'd left behind.

The song, his song, played in his head and swirled around in his memory. He recalled all the times when he felt distressed or sad, and he realized that he'd sought refuge in composing during those times.

"You gave me a whole lifetime to write a song," Brady said, speaking to himself as much as he was to the little man.

"Yes. Without a lifetime of experienced behind you, your sonata would be a lie." He then pointed to the piano. "Honor your family by finishing."

Moving with a grace and confidence that his body hadn't felt in ages, the now youthful Brady pulled up the bench and sat down. Did he feel anger? Sadness? Love? He wasn't even sure. He wiggled his fingers before placing them upon the keys. The sonata only needed a few finishing touches. Mostly he had to pin down a few chords in the last movement. Time stopped as Brady, who seemed to be immune from fatigue and hunger, ironed out every last detail of his masterpiece in the following hours, or possibly days.

"Done!" Brady shouted when every last note had found its home. He looked around, but the little man was nowhere to be found. Behind him a large door loomed. Fog rolled along the floor, eerily illuminated by light seeping in from under the threshold. He stood up and approached the door. A full-length mirror greeted him, which allowed him the opportunity to adjust the bowtie of the tuxedo he was all-of-the-sudden wearing. He smiled at the reflection of his twenty-seven-year-old self. When he was ready, the door opened to reveal the stage of an expansive concert hall, its seats filled with eager concertgoers. Their low murmur settled into complete silence as Brady stepped into the hall. A large grand piano sat center-stage.

Upon surveying the crowd, Brady spotted Carla at the center of the hall. She appeared as she did when they first met. She was flanked by their children and grandchildren. Behind her sat the little man with a large, excited smile upon his face. He made a motion with his hand, encouraging Brady to step to the piano. Brady did as he was told and sat down while a thousand patrons watched in anticipation. He placed his fingers on the keys. He played his life.

As the final notes faded out, the crowd gave an uproarious response—a two-minute standing ovation that made the walls shake. Tears formed in the eyes of Hollings. He made a bowing motion to Brady, which cued Brady himself to take a long bow. His children looked at him adoringly. He could see Carla mouthing, "I love you." Brady took it all in, right up until the moment when the sound of the crowd faded and was replaced by the sound of a woman screaming on the sidewalk below him.

Brady Hollis fell forty-seven floors and died.

THE BEAST OF THE RURZ VALLEY

The fur-covered beast stood on its hind legs and howled in anger. Merely ten feet away, thirteen-year-old Antonio stepped closer and raised his dagger. Had the beast not been held back by a chain staked to the ground, it surely would've charged the boy. Behind Antonio, a middle-aged man aimed a revolver at the beast's heart, though his finger was confidently off the trigger.

"Any second now," the man whispered, as if Antonio could hear him. "Whatever you do, don't turn your back to it."

Enraged by the youth who was carefully advancing toward him, the growling beast, twice as tall as the boy, pulled against the chain with all of its might. The iron links creaked, groaned, and then gave way with a sickening snap. The man with the gun, Magnus, could see Antonio tense up as the beast freed itself. He shifted his finger to the trigger, but a second later the boy's shoulders relaxed. *Yes, that's it,* Magnus thought. *Crouch low. Get under it.*

The beast moved quickly toward Antonio, but the boy, faster than most men, darted out of the way. A claw lashed out, but it caught only a few wisps of Antonio's hair as he went to his knee.

A smile graced Magnus's lips. *You've got him, boy,* he thought with satisfaction.

Rising up, Antonio thrust his dagger into the beast's stomach. He pushed upward with all of his strength until the silver tip of his dagger penetrated the heart. The creature looked skyward and howled in agony. Antonio pushed even harder on the butt of the knife, while warm blood from the creature dripped down his arm. A final, desperate slash came from the beast. Antonio dodged this attempt without even removing his hand from the knife. The creature gave one last pathetic wail and collapsed to the ground.

Antonio stood up proudly to his full height while Magnus stepped toward him and put his hand on his shoulder. Before them, the body of the creature began to transform. Its elongated nose and sharp teeth began to retract. Bones cracked as they reformed to their original shapes. The fur seemed to disappear, and the coal gray eyes took on a more pleasant shade of brown.

"Did you know the chain would break?" Antonio asked his mentor.

Magnus gave a knowing grin. "You must always be prepared for the unexpected," he said. He noticed Antonio frown. "I wouldn't have allowed it to happen if I didn't think you were ready for it," he added.

The naked body of a local farmer was laid out where the beast had fallen. "I knew this man," Antonio said matter-of-factly. "His name is Jonathan Franklin."

Magnus shook his head. "Jonathan Franklin died three months ago when he was attacked. This thing here is simply a remnant, a left-over from what he once was. That's something you must always remember, Antonio. These creatures have no humanity left, even during the daytime when they pretend to be who they once were. They're remorseless killers, sent by the devil himself."

The two of them left the body and walked onto the grounds of a nearby cathedral, which was surrounded by several comfortable-looking cottages. "Your father would be proud of you," Magnus commented to the boy. "You're already far braver and more skilled than any man in this province."

Antonio gave a rare smile. "Even you?"

Magnus held his fist up in mock anger. "Don't get cocky," he said with a laugh. "Let's go eat. Angelica has made us soup. Clean up before you join us."

Magnus disappeared into one of the cabins while Antonio washed off the blood in a trough of water. From the cathedral, two robed men exited and approached the body of Jonathan Franklin. Together, they carted the corpse to a graveyard and unceremoniously buried it.

TWENTY YEARS LATER

The residents of the Rurz Valley kept mostly to themselves. Antonio figured that there were maybe ten settlements that dotted the valley floor, with some small farms interspersed throughout.

He'd seen places like this before, and places like this weren't very special, although this particular valley had the distinction of being the hiding place of the final surviving creature. Somewhere, nestled between Alcander Peak and Hangman's Ridge, it roamed. This creature was desperate—it seemed to intrinsically know that it was the last of its kind. Three years earlier, its ilk had inhabited the hillsides and hollows in much greater numbers, but that was when Antonio rallied his team of hunters and drove them to greatness. They'd been far more successful than any of the teams that had come before them, even the teams headed by Magnus himself.

With a holy command from Cardinal Walster, the group had started their latest mission numbering five men and three dogs. Now, after several bloody encounters, they were down to only two men and one dog. But even with their losses, their successes had been far greater. Antonio had trained his men well, and he was relentless, absolutely relentless, in his pursuit. The team did their hunting at night, as the creatures themselves did.

At dawn, Antonio and his sole surviving human team member, Edmond, made their daytime camp just outside one of the valley's insignificant settlements. Unable to sleep, Edmond ventured into the town and returned two hours later accompanied by a young woman—even at that early hour he'd managed to find reasonably priced companionship. Antonio stared at him disapprovingly, even though he tacitly allowed such liaisons. *Let him have his moment of happiness. He can reckon with God on his own*, he thought. Billy the dog sniffed at the new arrival before circling and lying back down.

A few minutes later, various grunts and groans filled the campsite as Edmond and his new lover consummated their relationship. Antonio, in his bedroll, simply prayed. Soon the noises ceased, and a low conversation could be heard from the two temporary lovers.

"So, you hunt those wolf-men?" the female voice questioned.

"Yes. They're animal by night—human by day. They eat people to survive, but every once in a while, when their numbers thin, they allow someone to survive their attacks."

The woman listened with admiration. "Looks like I should give you another one for free," she said with a laugh. Before Edmond could agree, the woman perked up as she suddenly remembered something. "Wait! There was a man in town yesterday who said he was looking for a group of hunters like you."

"Who?" Edmond demanded.

"His name was… Mag-something."

Antonio shot up from his bedroll. "Magnus?"

"Yes! That's right, Magnus was his name. I think he's still in town."

Antonio shouted to the dog, "Billy, go find Magnus!"

Billy's ears perked up. His intelligent eyes narrowed as his snout raised and sniffed the air.

"Let's go," Antonio ordered. Edmond, struggling to get his pants on, stumbled as he tried to keep up with Antonio and Billy.

The dog homed in on Magnus in a matter of minutes, giving an excited yelp when he saw him walking outside one of the buildings.

"Magnus!" Antonio yelled to his mentor.

Magnus turned toward the men with a relieved smile on his face. "Thank God I found you! I was praying you would stop by this town."

The men greeted each other with an embrace. "You got my letter?" Antonio asked Magnus.

"Yes, and I've consulted with the Cardinal."

"And?"

"We believe that you're correct. This is the last one. There are no further reports of attacks anywhere."

Edmond came running up to them, still buttoning his shirt. "Did I hear him correctly? This truly is the last of the creatures?" he asked.

"Hello Edmond," Magnus said. "Yes, the beast you're current-ly tracking is the last of its kind, assuming you've been careful."

"There have been no survivors of its attacks," Antonio assured him. "It's desperate and injured. We'll soon have him."

"Injured? How so?"

"We already had a run-in with it. I put a dagger in its right eye," Antonio said as he made a stabbing motion. "Unfortunately, it managed to get away. That was two days ago."

Edmond nodded in agreement. "It doesn't have much fight left in it. We're honored that you came to witness our final victory."

"I came to make sure you two don't muck everything up. Car-dinal's orders."

"We're glad to have you," Antonio said earnestly, "but you al-ready know we'll succeed in our task."

A small smile broke through the creases in the older man's face. "You've far exceeded any expectations that we could've possibly had for you. No team has ever been this successful."

"Many friends have sacrificed their lives so that we could get to this point," Antonio said. "But for now, we're in need of rest if we're to continue the hunt."

"Of course you are," Magnus said. "You're camped outside of town, I assume. Gather your things and bring them here. I have a room at the inn we can share."

The two men did as Magnus instructed, hauling their belongings to the inn and making themselves comfortable. It was the first true rest either of them had gotten in months. They were woken late in the afternoon by Magnus. "I've had the innkeeper prepare us a meal," he told them. "Let's eat."

Antonio and Edmond rose from their slumber and joined Magnus in the tavern, where they ate a hearty soup. "It appears as if rest has suited you well," Magnus told the men as they ate. "Maybe you'd benefit from staying here another day."

Antonio put his spoon down and looked at Magnus oddly. "With all due respect, we'll get all the rest we need after we kill the beast."

"Of course," said Magnus.

Edmond thought he saw a look of annoyance flash across Antonio's face, but quickly decided that he'd imagined it. The suggestion wasn't made again, and the men finished their dinner while relaying the details of their most recent adventures to Magnus.

At sunset, the men and the dog, determined and ready, headed out into the woods. Antonio, leading them with an unwavering gait, pushed through the overhanging vines and the thickened brush. They kept their lanterns dim so as not to attract unwanted attention, and for an hour they walked in silence. Even their footsteps made no noise, so it was startling when Magnus abruptly broke the peace. "Are you sure we're headed in the correct direction?"

Antonio brushed off the suggestion that he was leading them down the wrong path. "I think you might be losing your eyesight." He pointed to a freshly broken branch that straddled the pathway. "The signs are clear."

"The creature wants to trick us. If I was him, I would double-back the other way," the older man said.

Antonio paused for a moment and stroked the stubble on his chin. "No. I've tracked this thing too long. I already know what it's going to do." He started walking again. "You're giving it too much credit."

"I suppose," Magnus said with a defeated sigh.

Antonio led them further into the valley, scanning the treelines and keeping his senses alert. Stopping suddenly, he held his arm out to signal the others to do the same. His head shifted to one side. "Do you hear that?" he asked. It's coming from that direction!" He pointed ahead of them.

Off in the distance, they saw a homestead illuminated in the moonlight. "Let's go!" Antonio said as he ran off toward the farmhouse with the other two following him. As they approached the structure, the three men drew their revolvers. Wordlessly, Antonio directed Edmond and Billy to go around to the backside of the two-room hovel. He nodded to Magnus, then pushed the door open with his foot. Inside, they could hear a raspy breath begging for air. Antonio increased the light from his lantern, and as he stepped in, the receding shadows revealed a bloody woman on the floor.

Magnus knelt down and tended to the woman while Antonio's gaze swept over the room. From his position, he was able to see into the back room. "There's a broken window back there. It must have left that way," Antonio said as he turned his attention to the woman on the ground. "Are her wounds fatal?"

"No," Magnus said. "These claw marks are deep, but he avoided her throat."

"That was intentional. This thing is trying to slow us down." From outside they could hear horses whinnying in the barn. Antonio knelt next to the woman and looked into her eyes. She was confused and delirious. Her black hair was pasted to her face with sweat. "I'm going to help you," he said as he grabbed her hand. With his other hand he compassionately stroked her face. The woman seemed to find solace in his words. "Be at peace," he said before abruptly withdrawing his silver tipped dagger from its sheath. The pace of the woman's breath quickened as she saw the weapon glint in the light of the lantern. Antonio held it above the woman and then quickly plunged it through her breastbone. She convulsed as the dagger sank deep into her chest. Antonio held the instrument firmly until she stopped moving.

Outside, Billy yelped frantically as the smell of his desperate quarry wafted from the barn. "Stand down, Billy!" Edmond ordered. Billy, anxious, mad, and unwilling to hold back any longer, ran off to the barn. Edmond attempted to follow him, but stopped as Billy entered the rickety building. The sound of Billy's growling was suddenly eclipsed by a much more menacing snarl. The barn door slammed shut as Billy yelped out in pain. He was quickly silenced with a nauseating crunch.

As Antonio and Magnus joined him outside, Edmond shook his head in sorrow.

Antonio sought to reassure his friend. "He's the last sacrifice we'll have to make."

Edmond nodded his agreement. "It will end tonight, but what I don't understand is why it's choosing to hide."

"It's the last stand of a desperate creature," Magnus responded. "It's tired of running. It means to lure us in."

"A desperate creature is the most dangerous," Antonio stated. "We will be careful, but we must press forward."

Antonio walked assuredly toward the barn, but Magnus stopped him with a firm hand on his shoulder. "Antonio, there will be no coming back from this."

Antonio turned to his mentor. "I've spent too many years getting to this point. After all my sacrifices—this is the last one!"

Edmond stared at the two other men, unsure why Magnus seemed so hesitant, but whatever it was, neither man elaborated on it further.

They continued their approach toward the barn. Their revolvers, each loaded with silver bullets, were at the ready. Antonio leveled his gun at the door and motioned to Edmond to open it. The door creaked as Edmond pushed on it. Blackness—the men could see nothing within the barn.

Behind them, Magnus reached into his pocket and removed a cyanide pill which he placed in his mouth, adjusting it so that it was securely in the pocket of his cheek and at-the-ready if he needed it. "It's not in there anymore. It must've run into the woods," he said.

Antonio shook his head and shushed the older man, all while feeling guilty at the disrespect he was showing his mentor. "It's in there!" he insisted. He motioned for Edmond to place his lantern on the ground. Once he did so, Antonio grabbed a nearby hoe and pushed the lantern inside, illuminating the interior.

"Well then, just burn the barn down and we'll shoot it when it runs out," Magnus said.

Antonio's annoyance flared, but he quickly found his respect again. "Not likely to work," he whispered to Magnus. "Waiting for it to smash through a wall of flame won't be to our advantage." He sighed at what he knew he had to say next. "Perhaps Magnus, it would be better if you waited out here." It emotionally wrecked him to suggest that his mentor stay back.

The older man stood motionless while the other two men stepped toward the barn and left him behind. "Lord, give me the strength to do what I must," Magnus whispered to himself. He raised his gun up in the direction of the other two, then, after a moment's contemplation, lowered it with a defeated sigh.

Oblivious to the crisis of conscience that was going on behind them, Antonio and Edmond peered inside the structure. Most of the light from Edmond's lantern was absorbed by its immediate surroundings, leaving a darkened periphery, but at least the men knew the creature wasn't waiting for them in the doorway. Each man took another step into the barn. A low growl from beyond the arc of light sounded out. Edmond pointed his gun at its source, but a moment later the same growling sound came from a different spot. The creature had moved quickly.

Antonio made a motion with his hand, instructing Edmond to move further into the barn. Edmond did so, leaving the relative safety of the lighted area. In the darkness, Edmond heard the growl again. He raised his gun and fired. The ignition of the gunpowder gave him a brief glimpse of the creature as it darted away. Edmond hadn't even come close to striking it. He started to step back.

"Stay there," came Antonio's firm command.

The growl pitched lower, then ceased completely.

Here it comes, Antonio thought. The creature would be smart enough to avoid the obvious temptation, and Antonio knew that it was he, not Edmond, who would be the monster's target—and that was the trap Antonio was setting. The only question, would it approach him from the left side or the right? In a fraction of a second, Antonio remembered the creature's injured right eye. By approaching from the left, it would be able to keep more of the barn within its view. He quickly turned to his left, and a split second later, a snarl could be heard coming toward him. Antonio fired his gun.

The bullet, well-aimed, tore through the creature's chest. Antonio ducked down as the beast careened over his head and landed with a thud behind him.

Edmond darted over and picked up his lantern. On the ground, the defeated beast could be seen taking heavy breaths. It tried to stand up but fell back down. It was done for.

Antonio took a brief moment to enjoy his triumph. He wasn't typically the type of person to savor victories, but this was the final one. It was a moment of pride for him. He turned to Magnus as the older man stepped into the barn. "We did it!" he said.

"It's a magnificent victory," Magnus replied, almost solemnly.

Antonio kept his gun on the beast. "Go finish him off, Edmond," he said to his friend.

"No, the privilege should be yours," Edmond said with deference.

"Okay then," Antonio said. "This will be it." He holstered his gun and removed his dagger as he moved toward his fallen foe.

Before he could take a step, the sorrowful voice of Magnus sounded out from behind him. "I wish you had listened to me just once tonight, Antonio. Know that I love you like a son."

Antonio had only a second to ponder the meaning of what Magnus had said before he felt a sturdy hand land on his shoulder and pull him backwards. A strong, stinging sensation moved from his back all the way through to his front side. Looking down, he could see the silver tip of Magnus's dagger erupting from his chest. A crimson stain formed on his shirt as the blood spurted forth.

"Traitor!" Edmond screamed as he rushed toward Magnus.

With his dagger still in Antonio's back, Magnus waited for Edmond to step closer and then knocked him unconscious with a single blow to his head.

Antonio's vision faded. Slowly, Magnus lowered him to the earth, taking great care to cradle his head. As he neared the ground, Magnus jerked the knife clean from his back so that Antonio could lie flat. He held the stricken man's hand while the pulse that ran through it weakened. Antonio's final view was that of his beloved mentor staring down at him with sorrow. His world, one of monsters and their victims, faded away from his thoughts.

"I didn't want this," Magnus said to the body lying before him.

Off to the side, Edmond began to stir. Magnus reached over and removed the other man's revolver before he could regain his senses. A moment later Edmond's eyes shot open, and with surprising quickness he pushed himself to a standing position. "What did you do?" he demanded of the older man once he was fully erect. "You'll be accountable for this!" He reached toward his holster but found it empty.

"Would you like this back?" Magnus asked with sincerity as he held up the firearm. Its barrel was pointed harmlessly at the ground.

"Right now I would very much like it back," Edmond said defiantly as he eyed the body of Antonio.

"Then give it back to you I shall. And have your revenge on me you shall, if that's what you desire, but first, there's something to take care of." He moved closer to the still-breathing creature. "Edmond, what is this creature's name?"

Edmond looked at him with an uncharacteristic boldness. "This creature is evil itself. It has no identity beyond that as far as I'm concerned."

"Its name!" Magnus ordered. "You've been tracking it. You know the name it uses when it walks by day. Tell me!"

Magnus could see the struggle within Edmond, who finally mumbled an answer, barely above a whisper. "Matthew."

"Speak up, Edmond!"

Edmond asserted himself. "Matthew. His name is Matthew."

"Thank you," the older man said, reverting to a kindly voice. He cautiously approached the stricken beast. Its bloody wound oozed and gaped as the creature rolled over to look at him. "Matthew!" he said while staring the beast in its good eye. "Can you understand me?"

The creature stared back at Magnus. Though it didn't directly acknowledge the question, the look of intelligence in the creature's eye gave Magnus enough confidence that it had at least a modicum of understanding.

"Remain still if you'd like me to help you," the older man said.

The creature let out a low, rumbling growl. Its mouth opened and saliva dripped from its jowls.

Magnus showed no fear. "You can attack me, but I won't be able to heal you."

Behind them, Edmond paced in anger as he gripped his dagger, contemplating which of the two would be his first target.

Magnus addressed Edmond without even turning around. "I must insist that you hold off on your revenge for a few more moments."

Edmond slipped his dagger back into its sheath, concluding he would most likely be bested by Magnus in a fight. Instead, he argued with the older man. "You're not going to heal it!" he said in an almost whiny tone.

"Not fully, but I won't let this creature die tonight."

Magnus reached two fingers into a leather pouch tied around his waist and removed a pinch of blue powder. He moved his hand over Matthew's wound and let a small amount of the powder fall into the hole. The wound sizzled and bubbled as Magnus stepped back from the creature.

"You deserve an explanation for this, my friend," Magnus said to Edmond.

"No friend of mine would perform the acts that I've just seen."

Magnus ignored Edmond's retort and continued, "Here's what you must understand—there was a time long ago when these creatures didn't exist, yet Satan felt compelled to create them. Do you know why that is?"

Edmond shook his head. "I never asked myself that question."

Magnus explained, "Three hundred years ago, before these wolves were ever spawned, an entirely different type of creature roamed the land. They, too, were physical manifestations of evil. They multiplied—they spread death and sadness throughout the known world! I can't tell you what they were called. I can't even tell you what they looked like—that's information that's privy only to the Cardinal."

"I don't see your point," Edmond said.

"What do you think happened to those creatures?"

Edmond thought hard. "They were hunted down, weren't they? Much like we hunt this creature."

"Yes," Magnus said. "You seem to be catching on. The creatures were hunted and destroyed, every last one of them over the course of a generation."

"That sounds like a good thing to me."

"But what the church didn't realize at the time is that these manifestations are like weeds—they can be plucked, but others will always grow back in their place."

Edmond's understanding grew as he listened to the older man talk.

Magnus continued, "This creature here is only an agent of Satan, and destroying the agent doesn't destroy the evil that constructed it, it simply creates a void that must be filled. So you see, we can either live with the manifestation that we already know, or be faced with something entirely new—a monster that we don't understand, and will likely be even more sinister."

"So, by letting this creature live, we avoid the creation of something worse?" Edmond let the weight of his question sink in.

"That's what the Cardinal believes, yes. History has shown that Satan will craft a monster even more nefarious to take its place. Our job should be only to keep the creatures in check—to keep their numbers low. But Antonio was too good, the best hunter in two-hundred years. Tonight he nearly caused their extinction." Magnus glanced at the stirring creature. "We should leave here; he'll be up and walking soon."

Edmond ignored the warning. "Then why didn't you have this conversation with Antonio? Why didn't you ask him to slow down? It wasn't necessary to kill him!"

"You think I didn't tell him this? I spoke to him about it many times, but he didn't believe me. He was too motivated, too determined, and too stubborn to stop what he was doing. He would've gone on hunting without the permission of the Cardinal if he had to. There was no stopping him."

The beast began moving as its wound slowly healed. A low growl could be heard coming from deep within.

"We should leave this area," Magnus once again insisted.

"No!" Edmond asserted. "I'm not yet convinced that what you say is true. Maybe the Cardinal is just afraid of losing his standing as a Holy Defender! Do you really believe him?"

"I must believe him," Magnus responded.

The creature's breathing steadied as it began to stand.

"We still have a chance to destroy it!" Edmond shouted. He dove over to Antonio's corpse and grabbed the dead man's revolver.

"Stand down!" Magnus shouted to Edmond.

Edmond ignored the direction and popped up to a kneeling position, his gun aimed straight at the creature's heart. But as quick as Edmond was, Magnus was quicker, and managed to raise his revolver and shoot first, putting a bullet through Edmond's calf. Edmond fell to the ground as he fired, his shot sailing harmlessly over the creature.

Magnus continued to train his gun upon Edmond, moving it along the outline of his body until it was pointed straight at his head. "I don't want to kill two men in one night."

The creature rose up to its full height, close enough to Magnus so that he could feel its moist breath dance across his cheek and into his ear canal. He knew if the beast moved to attack, he would have only a fleeting moment with which to put a bullet between Edmond's eyes. There could be no other way, the creature had to survive. He moved his cyanide capsule from his gums so that it rested between his molars.

"Matthew!" Magnus said, without turning away from Edmond. "Matthew, leave us!" The beast continued to cover the man with his breath, which smelled of rot. "Matthew, if you attack me this man will kill you," he said, hoping that the beast would buy his bluff.

Matthew lowered himself down to all fours and stepped over to Antonio's corpse. Then, after giving a defiant look back at Magnus, he bit down on the dead man's face. Magnus, who dared not turn from that direction, was forced to watch as Matthew's teeth crunched through the skull of his former pupil. The creature continued to bite down, spitting out the bone shards and brain matter.

At that moment, Magnus hated the creature more than he thought possible. He continued to watch as the beast moved toward Antonio's belly, where his claws ripped out the intestines. The creature ate no part of Antonio, taking time only to defile his corpse. The final insult was a warm stream of piss that drenched Antonio's remains. The beast Mathew stood up and gave a howl, then walked slowly past Magnus on two legs, rather than its typical four. "Leave now!" Magnus demanded. "You have your life."

The creature left the barn and disappeared down the path, dropping back to all fours as the fog enveloped him.

Edmond watched as Matthew disappeared. "There's a small hamlet in that direction. They're totally unprotected," he sighed.

"They're to be sacrificed for the greater good. There's nothing that can be done for them," said Magnus as he dropped the gun to the ground.

Edmond, after determining that Magnus had only given him a flesh wound, stood up. He faced the older man, and he saw the deep lines etched in his face. His tired eyes begged for sleep. He raised Antonio's revolver to the older man's head.

"It's okay, Edmond. I told you that you would have this opportunity. You have my forgiveness beforehand, if you feel you need it."

Edmond's hand shook, but he didn't pull the trigger.

Magnus continued, "My Angelica has been gone for ten years. I'm old, lonely. My body aches daily, and tonight, I was compelled to murder a man who was like a son to me. Please, do it."

Edmond lowered the gun. "You should just bite down on that capsule in your mouth if you're so determined to die."

Magnus frowned. "That's not something I would receive absolution for." He spit out the capsule. "If you're not going to end me, then at least help me bury Antonio."

The two men worked together to dig an appropriate grave for their fallen friend. The site was marked with a heavy rock and a cross that Edmond had carved from some wood. They both spoke their words of sadness and loss over the grave.

"What happens next?" Edmond asked as the impromptu ceremony ended. "Do we stop hunting the creature?"

"No," came the response. "You'll accompany me back to the cathedral. I want you to get a new team together. You're the lead hunter now. The beast will have time to recover, but more importantly, he'll have time to create others in his image."

"And what if I manage to hunt them all down again? Do you expect me to hold back?"

Magnus gave an unexpected smile and spoke. "You're not half the hunter that Antonio was. I expect that you'll use all of your skill and cunning. And with that, we'll achieve balance."

Edmond nodded his head in agreement. "When we take up the hunt again, we'll start with Matthew."

"Yes. He will be first," Magnus agreed. "I demand it." With that, the two men left the area, walking in the direction opposite from that of the creature.

CANDYBOOT

If you ever asked Candyboot to describe himself, the first thing he'd tell you is that he's devilishly handsome with an excellent sense of humor. He'd probably brag that he can speak every language known to man. He would add that he's polite, forgiving, and an overall great guy. If you let him go long enough, I'm sure he'd mention that he has friends all over the world who he loves to spend time with.

If you asked *me* to describe Candyboot, it would be a hell of a lot closer to the truth. I'd tell you that he's about two feet tall with a reddish Mohawk, sharp little teeth, and pointy talons. He's definitely *not* handsome. As for his sense of humor, some people might find him funny, as long as they're not the ones who are the butt of his pranks. The boast about speaking every language is most likely true, though his politeness exists only in spurts. And the claim about having friends all over the world? Well, he certainly has acquaintances, but I doubt that any of them would consider him a friend.

Candyboot is an imp, a sprite, or a gremlin—I don't really know what his species is, but what's certain is that he's a magical prankster of the most vicious sort. At best he's a nuisance, and at worst… well, you'll see shortly.

And that leads to me, Evan. I'm one of Candyboot's many worldwide acquaintances. He tells me that of all the people he stays with, I'm his favorite, but I suspect he says that to all of his "friends." His modus operandi is to jump from location to location, usually staying for no more than two weeks at a time in any one spot. If you're lucky, and if you catch him in the right mood, he can actually be very interesting and chatty (he's the reason I can swear in fifteen languages). I didn't choose to be one of his acquaintances—I want to make that much clear. He just showed up one day, telling me that I was to be congratulated on becoming his newest friend. That was ten years ago, when I was eight. It was terrifying the first time I saw him, but I won't go too much into that first meeting now—that story is best saved for another time.

I don't know why he picked me to be one of his hosts, and he never gives me a fixed response when I ask him. Once, he told me that it was because he heard me playing "bloody Mary" in the bathroom one day. "You called to me," he explained. I tried to argue that he was neither bloody nor named Mary. He just laughed. After a while, his answers became more and more ridiculous, so I stopped putting too much thought into the reason for our relationship.

The only thing that makes him somewhat tolerable is the shortness of his visits. He poofs in with a little cloud of smoke, stays two weeks or less, and then he's gone again, off to other corners of the world for months at a time. I suppose there's some unfortunate kid in China who has the same Candyboot problem that I have. I don't know how many "friends" he has, but I'm glad he spreads himself around.

By the way, when he's here, he only shows himself to me. When I was younger, I had a hell of a time trying to convince my mother that a little imp had been spending the past few nights sleeping on a pile of my dirty underwear. I finally gave up on that since he can go invisible at a moment's notice. In the end, it was easier simply to accept his presence and shut up.

He operates within some set of guidelines that I don't completely understand, scoring non-existent points when he pulls off a successful prank. "Ten points to me!" he said after magically changing my completed homework into a multi-page love note to my sixty-year-old teacher. I actually turned it in, thinking it was still my report on the Civil War. What followed was probably the most embarrassing parent-student-teacher conference ever. Another time, he woke me up by giving me a decidedly non-magical atomic wedgie. "Five points…" he huffed and puffed as he tried to pull my underwear over the back of my head. "Poin… points to me!" he said triumphantly, as he finally succeeded. For the most part though, he just skulks around mumbling to himself and getting into things. I try to ignore him, but it's hard when you're studying and you see him out of the corner of your eye using your toothbrush to style his nose hair.

I could go on and on about life with Candyboot, but it's easiest just to say that you get used to having him around—and as I already alluded to, sometimes he's not even that bad. If you ask nicely, he'll tell you all sorts of interesting stories about his brothers (he has fifty of them). So that's how it is with Candyboot, him popping in unannounced and uninvited, playing practical jokes, acting like a jackass, and then leaving. Rinse, repeat.

If you don't count Candyboot (and please don't), our household consists of me, my mother, and my little brother Kyle. Around this time last year, we were busy planning a party for my brother's tenth birthday. Candyboot had been out of the picture for several months at that point, and I prayed that he'd still be gone, at least until the party passed. As far as my little brother was concerned, I have to say, the little guy had really earned himself a big bash. For a long time, he'd been a bit of a pistol—it probably had something to do with my dad leaving. However, he'd gotten his grades up and the teacher was no longer sending home conduct reports, so my mom and I wanted to reward him. The party was going to be really kick-ass, with tons of people, a huge cake, a piñata, a bounce castle, and Pickles the Clown.

It was the night before the party when Candyboot returned. I have a sneaking suspicion that he knew about it all along, but he acted as if he had no clue what was going on. "What's this?" he demanded in his croaky voice only moments after magically appearing right next to me. I saw he was pointing at a paper mache horse.

"Hello, Candyboot," I said with a sigh. "It's a piñata. I can't believe you don't know what it is."

"Sé exactamente lo que es, idiota," came the hoarse reply.

"Then why did you ask me what… ya know, never mind."

Candyboot let out a cackle to let me know he was pleased with himself. He opened the box that held the cake. "What flavor is this?" he asked as his dirty little talon skimmed some frosting off the top.

"Get away from that!" I shouted as I shooed him away. He gave an excited chuckle and jumped up from the counter onto one of the rotating blades of the ceiling fan. "You can't have any!" I added as I closed the box back up.

Candyboot slowly licked the frosting that was still stuck to his talon. "Sweet," he commented. "We're going to have a good time tomorrow."

"Yes, that's right," I said. "WE—as in me, my mom, my brother, and all our guests. That doesn't include you." I spoke as if I could actually control Candyboot. I was praying that, just once, he'd sense that something was important to me and just leave. It. Alone.

Candyboot didn't acknowledge his uninvitation. "It's getting late," he said. "And anyway, I just came from Sweden. Jag tillbringade bara hela dagen jävla ett får." He yawned, exposing his dirty little teeth to all the world, then clapped his hands and disappeared in a cloud of smoke. Moments later, I could hear a tiny snore emanating from my bedroom.

I checked one last time on all the supplies. The decorations were already hung up. They looked great. I checked my email for the tenth time to make sure the catering was confirmed for the correct date. It was. I walked into my bedroom where I saw Candyboot lying across my bed, slowly humping my pillow in his sleep. I shook my head and pulled a spare blanket out of my closet, then, I laid myself on the floor and took way too long to fall asleep.

The next morning, I was woken by the sounds of the household. Kyle was talking excitedly, and my mother was setting up tables and chairs. Candyboot was nowhere to be found, though I knew he had to be close. I got dressed and joined my family as they set up. We were expecting about seventy guests—nearly all of Kyle's classmates and a bunch of our neighbors and friends.

The morning hours zipped by, and soon people began arriving. Pickles the Clown showed up and entertained the kids with magic. The younger crowd had fun in the bounce castle while the adults looked on in joy. It seemed that everyone was having a great time.

About an hour into the party, Candyboot made his reappearance. I'd spilled a little soda on my shirt and stepped into my bedroom to change. "How's it going out there?" the gruff voice asked from behind me.

I didn't even bother to turn around. "It's going great. Let's keep it that way."

"How old is that brother of yours?"

I wanted to ignore him, but I knew it was never wise to ignore the ignoble imp. "He's turning ten today."

"Hmmm." Candyboot stroked the few small beard hairs the dropped from his chin. "I never really liked him."

"Kyle? You don't even know him."

"I know him well enough," he shot back. "He's a bully. He hurts the other kids."

"He was acting out when my dad left," I responded, "but he's totally different now. That's why we're doing this for him." I could've said more, but I knew that it would be a waste of time to point out the irony of Candyboot being offended by a bully. "If you'll excuse me, I need to get back out there," I said as I high stepped over Candyboot.

"It's my birthday too, you know," Candyboot said.

I paused before reaching the door. "I didn't realize you had an actual birth. I thought you just… spawned out of a magical pile of garbage somewhere." It was a risky move to insult him, but the words felt good spilling from my mouth.

"My mother would be very unhappy to hear you say that, but I'm sure she'd forgive you if you threw me a party too."

"Okay." I paused, exasperated. "I'll do something for you tomorrow."

"It's not my birthday tomorrow."

"It's probably not even really your birthday today!" I argued.

"Yes it is. And if that bully is getting a party, I want one too. Right now."

"You want me to throw a party, in this bedroom, with just you and me, while the real party is going on out there?"

Candyboot nodded his pointy, gray head up and down.

"I can't do that, Candyboot. I have to help my mom run things out there." I opened the door and took a step into the hallway.

"Don't leave," he said slowly. I took another step out the door, determined not to be pushed around. His voice lowered. "Don't think you can insult my mother and then simply walk away. You'll regret it."

"I'm not going to let you push me around," I said. Standing tall, I walked out of the room, proud of my own determination. But then, before I could close the door behind me, I heard his little bony hands clap together two times. Magic—he'd just done something magical. I stepped back inside and closed the door, expecting to find Candyboot grinning and laughing to himself at whatever prank he'd just pulled. What I saw was much more concerning, Candyboot looked completely spent. Instead of his healthy gray patina, his skin was almost completely white. His eyes drooped, he was breathing heavily, and his dog-like ears pointed toward the ground.

What you have to know about Candyboot is that whenever he performs magic, it always takes a physical toll on him. The greater the magic, the bigger the toll. I'd never seen him look so bad. Whatever he had just done, it was something BIG.

I stomped over to him. "What did you just do?" I demanded.

A chuckle, interrupted by a cough, was his only response.

In anger, I grabbed his bony little arm and pulled him to me. "Tell me!"

Despite his drained state, he responded in inhumanly quick fashion. His free arm lashed out and slashed me directly below my elbow, his claws tearing deeply into my skin. I released my grip on him and screamed out in pain.

Candyboot's face was in a snarl. I must've had a look of absolute fear on my own face. His eyes shifted to my bleeding arm and his snarl slowly dissipated. Blood ran down to my fingers and dripped onto the carpet. I could only stare at him in shock. Nothing like that had ever happened between the two of us. Without a word, he clapped his hands together twice, and I felt a jolt go through my injured arm. When I looked down, I saw that the bleeding had stopped, and scabs had begun to form over the cuts. It wasn't completely healed, but it was no longer a serious injury.

At that point, Candyboot was completely wiped out. He fell over backwards and landed with a dusty little thud. Then, while making little grunting noises, he rolled over and crawled to my closet. The door was ajar, and with his last bit of energy he pulled it open and climbed up a pile of my dirty laundry. "Spero vi piacciano gli insetti," he said to me with the last of his wakefulness. "It's going to be sweet. One-thousand points to Candyboot." He gave a weak chuckle as he shaped a pair of my underwear into a tiny pillow. Then, he passed out. His little snores echoed around my room.

I took off my T-shirt and put on a long-sleeve shirt in its place. The sounds coming from the rest of the house indicated that everyone was still having a good time. Candyboot's prank, whatever it was, hadn't been unleashed yet. I stepped out into the hallway and looked around. There was Aunt Chloe with a soda in her hand. The neighbors were eating some pizza, children were running around laughing. Pickles the Clown was juggling some balls for the amusement of the smaller kids. Nothing seemed amiss.

I cautiously walked around, examining every corner and nook. I thought back to the last thing he said to me. *It's going to be sweet.* It was a clue. Sweet. Like cake maybe. I turned around and looked at the birthday cake. It was a huge single layer sheet, big enough so that everyone could have a piece. I have to say, it was a visual masterpiece of colorful icing and decoration. As far as I could tell, it was untouched, but Candyboot's magic wouldn't have left any outward signs. I ran through scenarios in my mind, envisioning that anyone who ate it would be cursed immediately with explosive diarrhea, which is exactly the kind of thing that Candyboot would find funny. There wasn't really time to think of a good plan, but I knew I had to get rid of it before it came time to serve it.

"Hey Mom," I shouted across the room, "don't you think we should have the cake on the other table?" I pointed over to the card table that had been set up in the living room.

My mother looked confused. "What? No, leave it where it is!"

"No mom, I think more people can enjoy looking at it if I move it over there."

With some effort, I picked up the cake and started walking. My mom's exasperated voice carried over the sounds of the party. "Just—just leave it. Be careful! BE CAREFUL!"

As my mom spoke her final warning, I feigned a stumble and dropped the cake to the floor. For good measure, I fell forward and landed on top of it.

The party became eerily silent. Seventy people—all looking at me with their jaws agape. Heck, even Pickles looked upset, which, if you can imagine, was especially difficult with his painted-on smile. I rolled myself off of the cake, further flattening it and removing any hope that it could be salvaged. Tiny bits of frosting had made their way into my mouth. They tasted delicious, but I had no choice but to spit them out.

"Evan!" my mom yelled as she stormed up to me. "What were you thinking?"

I apologized, and then apologized four more times, but my mom barely paid attention.

"Kyle, go grab some cleaning supplies," she said to my brother as she pointed under the kitchen sink. "Chloe, can you help me with this?" she asked my aunt. She turned to the children who had gathered around to witness the idiot who had dropped the cake.

"Why don't you kids go start the piñata? There's still more pizza, everyone!"

With my mom taking charge, the party started coming back to life. I looked like a fool, but secretly I considered myself a hero. My mother instructed me to go buy another cake, which I readily agreed to.

With frosting and cake all over my shirt, I returned to my bedroom to change yet again. Candyboot was still passed out in the closet. I thought about giving him a good swift kick, but then I thought better of it. I put on a clean shirt and returned to the festivities, where my mom handed me some cash. "Get enough for everyone," she said tersely. "Don't take too long."

I walked through the living room to where the last few remnants of cake were being cleaned up by a few of my relatives. The cake, though smashed, didn't look as though it'd been affected by any magic. My aunt Chloe got some frosting on her fingers, and I watched as she absent-mindedly licked it off. It seemed to have no effect on her, and I suddenly didn't feel very confident that the cake was the center of Candyboot's plan. "Sweet," I repeated to myself. What else at the party was sweet?

Everything seemed to move in slow motion as I looked around the room, taking in all the sights. Looking into the den, I could see a large space had been cleared out. The piñata had been strung up over one of the exposed beams along the vaulted ceiling. My uncle Joe was manipulating it, moving it up and down as a hapless small child took a swing at it with a bat. The child took one final swing before my brother Kyle stepped up and took a turn. He put the blindfold on, but even from across the room I could see he didn't really pull it all the way over his eyes. Cheater. As my uncle pulled on the rope to move it up, I saw the piñata momentarily bulge along its midsection, as if something inside of it was pushing out.

I screamed at Kyle to stop, but he either didn't hear me or didn't care. He stepped into his swing, like he'd been taught in little league, and nailed that damn piñata square in the middle. A large crunching sound erupted as the paper horse split open. Children, with their greedy little hands stretched out, pushed forward in anticipation of the sweets about to pour forth.

At first, I couldn't tell what it was that came spilling out of the piñata. For a half second, it looked like a single, black, pulsating blob that came falling to the floor, but as it descended, it began to spread out, and its individual elements became identifiable. Spiders, cockroaches, centipedes. All sorts of creepy things. Thousands of them. They hit the ground and immediately spread out like a ton of marbles rolling away from each other.

The children closest to the scene saw exactly what was happening, but as they tried to escape, they were pushed even closer by the clueless children behind them. This continued for a few seconds until it became clear to everyone that there were no sweets to be had. Soon they all pushed back, trying to leave the scrum that had formed around the busted piñata. Screams moved through the room as the bugs began crawling up the legs of the partygoers. I could hear my uncle Joe cuss and yell out, "Oh my God!" as he fell down. Several roaches crawled over his face.

The chaos spread as the disgusting bugs and panicked children fled from the den into the other rooms of the house. Pickles the Clown tried to maintain a sense of calmness. "Slow down, everyone," he said in a surprisingly calm voice. The kids paid no attention and trampled over him in their haste to exit the house. All I could see of him were his hands and legs shooting into the air as the kids stepped on his torso. A handful of the party goers rolled on the ground in an attempt to squash the bugs that had crawled into their clothing, though this had the unintended consequence of allowing even more bugs access to their internal compartments. A teenage girl tried to dive through a closed window in an attempt to get away, but she nearly knocked herself unconscious when the unyielding window proved to be a hell of a lot stronger than she anticipated. Bugs overran her as she sprawled out on the floor. People tripped, fell, and pushed each other. I somehow managed to avoid being knocked down.

Soon, the house was empty of people, with the exception of me, Pickles and a couple of others. Pickles moaned as he rolled over from his back and got onto his hands and knees. Somehow in the melee he'd swallowed his red foam nose, which he vomited up with a retching sound as bugs continued to run by him. Outside, people were stripping their clothes off and shaking out the bugs.

The moaning sounds of the fallen were punctuated by the hiss of a Madagascar cockroach that crawled up on the table behind me. I surveyed the scene, and, as far as I could tell, nobody was seriously injured. People had bumps, bruises, and cuts—things that would heal in relatively quick fashion. The psychological damages? Those wouldn't heal for a long time, if ever.

From my location, I could look down the hallway to my bedroom. The door opened slowly, and I made eye contact with Candyboot as he poked his head out. He gave a big smile as a wallet-sized spider walked past him and into my room. In his left hand he held the shirt I'd been wearing when I fell on the cake. He licked some frosting off of it, then raised it up and nodded to me as if he was making a toast. I nodded back to him, thoroughly defeated. *Happy birthday, you little fucker,* I thought. Candyboot dropped the shirt and made a thumbs up motion, then he clapped his hands together and disappeared, leaving a little puff of smoke in his wake.

He was gone, off to some other part of the world to spread his miserable little brand of humor. At least his visit had been a short one. I did a little dance-step to avoid a potato bug that had crawled up to me. As I brought my heel down on its body, I imagined that it was Candyboot. The crunching sound made me feel a little better. With that, I went over and helped Pickles up from his hands and knees, and together we went outside, away from the mess that Candyboot had created.

GOING HOME

It was the last rainstorm of his life; he already knew it. Staring out of his bedroom window at the retirement home, the old man gave a silent prayer of thanks for the late season downpour. If he was going to act, this was his last chance, ever.

With shaky hands, he zipped up his sweater and shuffled to the door of his room. He hesitated before stepping into the hallway, but only for a second. *I'm not chickening out, not this time*, he thought as he stepped through the threshold with a boldness he hadn't felt in decades. The door swung closed behind him with a solid click. He never looked back.

His steps grew more certain as he made his way into the reception area, where Enrique's booming voice greeted him. "Mr. Cooper, what are you doing awake at this hour?"

The old man, James Cooper, looked up and smiled. "Oh, I just had a little trouble sleeping."

Enrique noticed the sweater. "Is your room too cold?" He held out his hand to assist James. "Let's get you back to bed, I'll help you with your thermostat. Those digital models can be tricky."

"Oh, that would be nice," James said. "But first, could you get me a couple of extra blankets?"

"I'd be happy to. I'll meet you at your room in just a couple of minutes."

Enrique started to head off, but James stopped him with a hand on his shoulder. "I just want you to know, Enrique, you've always been my favorite staff here. You're a very kind man, and I've enjoyed our conversations over the years."

"Why thank you, Mister Cooper. That means a lot to me." Enrique was obviously touched.

"And," James continued, "I want to apologize in advance."

Enrique's face crunched up in bewilderment. "You don't have anything to apologize for. I'm always happy to help you."

"I know you are," James said. He began walking in the direction of his room, but stopped as soon as he saw Enrique leave the area. He had only moments to act. Making his way to the reception desk, he pulled open the drawer where he knew Enrique stored his personal keys. He found them in seconds. Looking over his shoulder to make sure Enrique was still out of sight, James pocketed the keys and shuffled over to the front doors, which opened automatically for him.

Bitter cold—the stinging wind smacked him in the face. He thought for a moment about returning, but resolved himself to move forward. As he cleared the awning, the hard raindrops began soaking his clothes. Behind him, the illuminated sign for the Abbey Bonita Retirement Center cast a pale glow into the parking lot. His eyesight was already poor, but the rain made it all that much more difficult to see. He knew that Enrique drove a big white car. After shuffling around the parking lot for far too long, James found his target. He held the key fob up and pushed one of the buttons. The car in front of him chirped. Success! James hobbled over to the vehicle and opened the door.

Once inside, he put the key in the ignition and turned the car on. Shivers ran through his body as the wetness soaked through his clothes and chilled his skin. He looked to turn on the heater, but with all the lights, gizmos, and switches, he couldn't figure out which controls to use. There was even a small video screen that confused the hell out of him. He'd given up his license fifteen years earlier, and even then his vehicle had been twenty years old. *When the hell did cars get so complicated?* he wondered.

Running low on time, he gave up trying to find the heater and decided to just make the best of it. He put his seat belt on and shifted into reverse. The car moved out of its parking space, and seconds later he felt the vehicle softly collide with another parked car.

"Oops. Sorry," James said to no one in particular.

He managed to put the car in drive and moved slowly through the lot. Leaning forward, he plastered his face against the inside of the windshield just so he could see. *Just like riding a bike,* James thought as the car meandered over the asphalt. He pulled out of the parking lot and headed down the empty street at no more than ten miles an hour. The next few miles were traveled in silence as the car repeatedly drifted in and out of its lane.

By the time he got to the Old River Bridge, he was shivering. Whether it was from the bitter cold or from his growing feeling of apprehension, he wasn't sure. He allowed the car to roll to a stop to give himself a chance to gather his nerve, then tapped the accelerator once he felt ready.

He gasped when he finally saw the figure. She had an almost glowing aura, though it was really just the headlights reflecting the rain falling around her. The car inched up to the moving figure and stopped.

Blue jeans, white t-shirt, no jacket—the girl was freezing. With a sorrowful look, she peered into the car. James scooted over and cracked the door for her. He could hear his heart beating.

The frigid little thing pulled the door open and sat inside. She stared straight ahead. "Thank you. I need to get home."

As cold as he already was, James noticed that the temperature dropped even lower when the girl entered. It was freezing in there. He could only stare at the sight of the specter next to him. The girl, who looked about seventeen, didn't seem to pay attention, but only repeated herself. "I need to get home."

"Horrible night, isn't it?"

The girl only nodded in response.

James took his foot off the brake, and the car gave a slight jerk before rolling forward. He'd imagined this moment for so long, he thought he knew what he would say when the time finally came, but they drove in silence with his practiced monologue nestled uselessly in a forgotten portion of his brain.

He finally found some words. "You were in a crash." It hadn't been his plan to start off that bluntly.

"I just need to get home."

"I know you do."

The girl gave no further response while the man struggled with what to say next. "You... your car went off the road and into the river, on a rainy night, just like tonight." His voice was shaking.

"Please, I just need to get home."

"Don't you remember?"

The girl shivered in silence as she continued to stare straight out the window.

James continued, "there have been so many stories over the years… at first I didn't believe them. I always thought the people telling them were just a bunch of crazy hippies high on LSD, but they always said the same thing. They spoke about the pretty girl with the reddish hair that was walking out in the rain, the girl who just wanted to get home."

An oncoming car screamed by, blaring its horn as James barely pulled back into his own lane in time. When he was finally able to stop shaking, he started his story again. "People would give her a ride, but she always disappeared right before they made it to her home. Some of them would even go and knock on the door to see if she had made it safely inside, but she never did."

The girl acted as if she hadn't heard a word of what he'd just said. "I just need to get home," she replied.

"I know you do, my Strawberry."

Strawberry—the girl realized it'd been ages since she'd been called that. Turning toward her driver for the first time, the girl stared intently at the man next to her. It took a few moments, but eventually she saw past the wrinkled skin and noticed the true shape of the man's face. She knew who he was. "Dad?"

He turned and faced her. "Yes, it's me."

"What happened? I don't understand!" A sudden panic overtook the poor girl. "What's going on?" She fumbled with the door handle in a clumsy attempt to open it and run out into the night.

"No!" He grabbed her and felt a shock of angry cold run up his arm. "It's okay. You're okay now."

She stopped struggling and sat with her eyes fixed straight forward, watching the rain hit the windshield. She nodded her head up and down. "I remember now. I slid off the road and into the river. The water filled up the car. It was so cold—and it's still cold."

"It's been fifty years, Strawberry. I don't want you to be cold any longer." The car pulled off the road and onto a long driveway that had long since been claimed by weeds. "Here we are," James said as the car stopped. At the top of the driveway sat a derelict house. Decades had passed since anyone had lived there, yet it was the same home the girl had been desperately trying to reach for so many years. "I'm sorry it took me so long to find you. I guess I was scared of what might happen, but I know now I had nothing to fear."

"Oh Dad," the girl said as she went to hug her father. The man felt the warmth of her embrace.

The police found his body the next morning, parked near an old house he'd lived in decades earlier. Hypothermia—that was the coroner's final conclusion, though she noted that the man had a whole list of ailments, any one of which would've likely killed him within a year. The coroner also noticed that he seemed to have died with a smile on his face, though that tidbit never made it into the final report.

As for the phantom hitchhiker, her legend, like any other good legend, never died. Whenever there was a storm, it seemed like there was always someone insisting afterward that they had picked her up on the side of the road. But those who made the claim were typically braggarts, liars, and attention-seekers. The real truth is that the girl, who'd spent half a century trying to return home, was never seen again.

www.ingramcontent.com/pod-product-compliance
Lightning Source LLC
Chambersburg PA
CBHW021559310726
48972CB00003B/864

9 781963 107067